If you think life settles into happy harmony after marriage, you may wish to reconsider before diving into this story. For Nirmala, the journey has just begun, and it is neither simple nor sweet. What lies ahead is not the fairy-tale romance we are accustomed to, but the struggle of a young bride trying to find meaning and connection in a relationship forged by obligation and social expectation. Dive in, if you dare, but be ready for the rawness of real emotions and unfulfilled desires.

Authored by: Premchand

Translated by: Surendra Singh

Edited by: Ashok Sharma (Senior Advisor)

Bhartiya Shiksha Shodh Sansthan,

Saraswati Kunj, Nirala Nagar Lucknow-20

First Edition: 2024

ISBN: 978 81 962264 9 7

# Nirmala

## Chapter - 1

*If you are expecting a happy and carefree childhood tale, you might be disappointed. If you are interested in happy endings, you would be better off reading another book. This story does not promise fairy-tale endings or unending joy. Instead, it delves into the bittersweet moments of a young girl's life as she navigates the complexities of growing up, revealing the burdens of family expectations, the loss of innocence, and the harsh realities of womanhood. However, if you are in search of stories that conclude with blissful endings, I urge you to look elsewhere.*

Babu Udaybhanulal's family was large, filled with cousins, nephews, and other relatives, but they aren't important to our story. He was a successful lawyer, fortunate in life, and he felt it was his duty to support the less fortunate members of his family. Our story is about his two daughters, Nirmala and Krishna. Just yesterday, they were playing with their dolls, creating stories and dreams with innocent hands. Nirmala was fifteen and Krishna ten, yet their hearts were the same, full of playfulness and joy. They loved adventures, no matter how small, and organized grand weddings for their dolls, all while skillfully avoiding any household chores. When their mother called them, her voice echoing through the house, they would hide on the terrace, not wanting to be caught for some task. They argued with their brothers, scolded the servants, and rushed to the door whenever they heard music that promised some fun.

But today, something had changed. Nirmala, the elder sister, suddenly found herself stepping into the role of an adult, while Krishna stayed in her innocent childhood. Krishna was still the same, but Nirmala had become quiet, serious, and shy. For the past few months, Babu Udaybhanulal had been searching for a suitable match for Nirmala. Today, his efforts had finally paid off. A match had been found with Babu Bhalchandra Sinha's eldest son, Bhuvanmohan Sinha. The groom's father kindly said that they didn't need to worry about dowry, but the hospitality for the wedding guests should be perfect to avoid any embarrassment.

Babu Udaybhanulal was a good lawyer, but he wasn't great at saving money. The dowry had been a big worry for him, so when the groom's father said there were no demands, it felt like a weight had been lifted from his shoulders. He had worried that he might need to beg from others and had even arranged with a few moneylenders. He had estimated that, even with being careful, the expenses would be at least twenty thousand. So, with this assurance, he felt a joy he hadn't felt in a long time.

The news left Nirmala sitting alone in a corner, her face covered, lost in her thoughts. A strange fear had taken hold of her, filling her heart with an unknown dread. She didn't know what to expect. There were no happy feelings, no excitement in her heart like young girls usually have — no shy glances, no sweet smiles, no relaxed joy. There were no dreams, just fears, worries, and timid thoughts. The full joy of youth had not yet come to her.

Krishna knows some things, but some remain a mystery to her. She knows that her sister will receive beautiful jewelry, drums will play at the door, guests will arrive, and there will be dancing — all of this fills her with joy. But she also knows that her sister will hug everyone, cry, and leave, and that she will be left alone — this makes her sad. However, she doesn't understand why this is happening, why their parents are so eager to send her sister away. Her sister hasn't done anything wrong, hasn't fought with anyone. Will they send her away like this one day too? Will she also sit alone in a corner, crying, with no one showing her any pity? This thought fills her with fear.

It was evening, and Nirmala sat alone on the terrace, gazing longingly at the sky with tired eyes. She wished she had wings so she could fly away, far from all the troubles. At this time, the two sisters would usually go for a walk. If the carriage wasn't available, they would stroll in the garden. Krishna was searching for her sister, and when she couldn't find her anywhere, she climbed up to the terrace. Seeing

Nirmala, she smiled and said, "Here you are, hiding while I've been looking everywhere for you. Come on, I've got the carriage ready."

Nirmala replied indifferently, "You go, I don't want to go."

Krishna insisted, "No, my dear sister, please come today. Look, how cool the breeze is."

Nirmala sighed, "I really don't feel like it, you go on."

Krishna's eyes filled with tears. In a trembling voice, she said, "Why won't you come today? Why won't you talk to me? You keep hiding away. I feel so restless sitting alone. If you won't go, then I won't either. I will stay here with you."

Nirmala looked at Krishna with a faint smile and said, "And what will you do when I'm gone? Who will you play with and who will you go out with then?"

Krishna replied, "I will go with you. I can't stay here alone."

Nirmala smiled, "Mother won't let you come with me."

Krishna insisted, "Then I won't let you go either. Why don't you tell Mother that you don't want to leave?"

Nirmala sighed, "I am telling her, but no one listens."

Krishna asked, "Isn't this your home too?"

Nirmala shook her head sadly, "No, if it were my home, why would they be so eager to send me away?"

Krishna whispered, "Will I be sent away like this too one day?"

Nirmala nodded, "Yes, we girls don't really have a home."

Krishna asked, "What about Chander? Will he be sent away too?"

Nirmala replied, "Chander is a boy; no one will send him away."

Krishna said, "Then girls must be really bad, right?"

Nirmala's eyes filled with sadness, "If we weren't bad, why would they drive us away?"

Krishna said, "Chander is so naughty, yet no one drives him away. We never do anything wrong."

Suddenly, Chander came stomping up the stairs and, seeing Nirmala, said, "Oh, here you are! Oh-ho, soon the drums will play, sister will become a bride, riding in a palanquin, oh-ho!"

Chander's full name was Chanderbhanu Sinha. He was three years younger than Nirmala and two years older than Krishna.

Nirmala warned him, "Chander, if you tease me, I'll go tell Mother right now."

Chander laughed, "Then why do you get annoyed? Just listen to the drums. Oh-ho! You're going to be a bride. Right, Krishna? You'll hear the drums too! You've never heard drums like these before."

Krishna asked, "Better than the band?"

Chander nodded enthusiastically, "Yes, yes! A thousand times better, a million times better! You heard one band and thought nothing could be better. The musicians will wear bright red uniforms and black caps. They'll look so handsome, you can't even imagine. There'll be fireworks too, rockets shooting up into the sky, reaching the stars, and then red, yellow, green, blue stars will fall down. It'll be amazing."

Krishna's eyes widened, "And what else, Chander? Tell me more, dear brother."

Chander smiled, "Come with me for a walk, and I'll tell you everything on the way. There'll be such wonders that your eyes will be wide open. Fairies flying in the sky, real fairies!"

Krishna jumped up, "Alright, let's go! But if you don't tell me, I'll hit you."

Chander and Krishna left, but Nirmala remained alone. Seeing Krishna leave at this moment made her feel deeply hurt. Krishna, whom she loved more than her own life, had become so indifferent today, leaving her all alone. It wasn't much, but a wounded heart is like a sore eye, where even the slightest breeze causes pain. Nirmala sat crying for a long time. She thought, my siblings, my parents — everyone will forget me like this. Their eyes will turn away, and perhaps, I will long just to see them again.

The garden was in full bloom, the sweet scent of flowers filled the air. The cool, gentle breeze of spring was blowing, and the sky was scattered with stars. Lost in her sorrowful thoughts, Nirmala fell asleep, and as soon as her eyes closed, her mind began to wander in the dream world. She found herself standing beside a river, waiting for a boat. It was dusk, and darkness was spreading like a terrifying creature. She was filled with anxiety, wondering how she would cross the river, how she would reach the other side. She was crying, fearing that night would fall, and how could she stay alone here then?

Suddenly, she saw a beautiful boat coming toward the shore. She leaped with joy, and as soon as the boat reached the bank, she moved forward to step into it. But as soon as she tried to set foot on the boat, the boatman said, "There is no place for you here!" She pleaded with him, fell at his feet, and cried, but he kept repeating, "There is no place for you here." In a moment, the boat began to sail away. She screamed and cried, thinking how she would spend the night alone on the desolate riverbank. She tried to jump into the river to catch the boat, but just then, a voice called out, "Stop, stop, the river is deep, you will drown. That boat is not for you, I am coming. Get into my boat, and I will take you across."

Terrified, she looked around to see where the voice was coming from. After a while, she saw a small dinghy approaching. It had no sail, no oar, and no mast. The bottom was cracked, planks were broken, and water was filling in, while a man was trying to bail it out. She said to him, "This boat is broken, how will it take me across?" The boatman replied, "This is the boat sent for you, come and sit." She hesitated for a moment — should she sit in it or not? In the end, she decided to sit. It was still better to sit in the boat than to stay here alone, she thought. It was better to drown in the river than end up in the belly of some wild creature. Who knows, the boat might make it across. With this thought, she boarded the boat, holding her breath.

For a while, the boat wobbled, but every moment it filled with more water. She started bailing out water with both hands, along with the boatman. Eventually, their hands grew tired, but the water kept rising. Finally, the boat began to spin, and it seemed like it was about to sink. She stretched out her hands, hoping for some invisible help. The boat started to go under, and her feet slipped. She screamed loudly, and at that very moment, her eyes opened. She found her mother standing in front of her, shaking her shoulder.

## Chapter - 2

*If you are hoping for moments of joy and celebration, you might want to turn the page to another story. Here, the shadow of responsibility looms over every fleeting smile, and the burden of expectations weighs down even the lightest of hearts. The world we step into is far from perfect, and the ending may not be as happy as you would hope.*

Babu Udaybhanulal's house had turned into a bustling marketplace. In the veranda, the goldsmith's hammers clanged, while inside the rooms, the tailor's needles were busy at work. Under the neem tree out front, a carpenter was making cots. In the courtyard, a makeshift stove had been set up for the confectioner. Another house had been arranged for the guests. The arrangements were such that every guest would have a cot, a chair, and a table. It was being planned that there would be one servant for every three guests. Though there was still a month left for the wedding, preparations were already in full swing. The idea was to treat the wedding guests so well that no one would have anything to complain about — to leave such an impression that they would remember this wedding forever.

The entire house was filled with utensils — tea sets, plates for snacks, trays, pitchers, and glasses. Those who usually spent their days lounging on beds, smoking hookahs, were now busily engaged in the work. It was a rare opportunity for them to prove their usefulness, something they hadn't had in a long time. Where one person was needed, five would rush to help. There was less work and more chaos. Every little thing led to long arguments, and in the end, Babu Udaybhanulal would have to come and settle the matter. One person would say, "This ghee is bad." Another would counter, "If you can find better in the market, I'll gladly walk away right now."" A third would add, "This smells rancid." A fourth would retort, "Your nose must be rotten! Do you even know what real ghee is? Ever since you arrived, you've actually had ghee; before that, you couldn't even dream of seeing it!" The argument would escalate until Babu Udaybhanulal had to step in and resolve it.

It was nine o'clock at night. Udaybhanulal sat inside, calculating the expenses. He did this almost every day, but every day there were changes, adjustments, or additions to be made. In front of him stood Kalyani, frowning. After a long while, Babu Udaybhanulal looked up and said, “It won't be less than ten thousand, perhaps even more.”

Kalyani said, "In ten days, the expenses have gone from five thousand to ten thousand. At this rate, by the end of the month, it might even reach a lakh."

Udaybhanulal sighed, "What can I do? We cannot afford to let people ridicule us. If anyone complains, they'll say we only have a name but no substance. Besides, when they are not asking for a single penny in dowry, it is my duty to make sure the guests are treated with the utmost respect."

Kalyani shook her head, "Since the beginning of time, no one has ever been able to fully satisfy a wedding party. They will always find something to criticize. Even someone who struggles to get dry bread at home turns into a tyrant when they are part of a wedding party. The oil isn't fragrant enough, the soap seems like it was picked up from some cheap store, the servants don't listen, the lanterns give off smoke, the chairs have bedbugs, the cots are shaky, and the guesthouse isn't airy enough. There are a thousand complaints like these. How can you possibly address all of them? If they don't get this chance, they'll find other flaws. They'll say, 'This oil is only fit for courtesans; we want plain oil,' or 'This soap isn't good enough; they've sent this just to show off their wealth, as if we've never seen soap before.' 'These servants are like demons, always hovering over our heads!' 'The lanterns are so bright that they'll make you blind if you sit near them for a few days.' 'The guesthouse is like a cursed place, with drafts coming in from all sides.' I'm telling you, just forget about trying to satisfy these guests."

Udaybhanulal asked, "Then what do you want me to do?"

Kalyani replied, "I've been saying, make a firm decision not to spend more than five thousand. We don't even have the money at home; it's all based on loans. Why take on so much debt that we can never repay it in this lifetime? We have other children too; we need to think of their future as well."

Udaybhanulal said, "So, am I supposed to just die today?"

Kalyani responded, "No one knows what tomorrow holds."

She continued, "There's no point in getting upset about it. Everyone has to die one day; no one is here forever. Ignoring the inevitable won't make it go away. I see it every day — a father passes away, and his children are left wandering from street to street. Why should a person set themselves up for such a fate?"

Udaybhanulal retorted angrily, "So, should I take this as a prophecy that my end is near? I never thought a wife would grow tired of her husband's presence, but it seems I've learned something new today. Perhaps widowhood has its own charms!"

Kalyani shot back, "Whenever anyone tries to have a sensible conversation with you, all you do is spew venom. Is it because you think I have nowhere else to go, and that I am dependent on you for every meal? The moment I say anything, you act like I'm nothing more than a servant here, that my role is just to cook and clean. The more I back down, the more you press. It's fine if freeloaders waste our money, fine if it goes on drinks and feasts, but the moment I speak up, I become the villain. All the sacrifices are for my children to bear."

Udaybhanulal snapped, "So, am I your slave?"

Kalyani countered, "And am I your servant?"

Udaybhanulal scoffed, "I am not that person who dance to the whims of their wives."

Kalyani retorted, "And i am not that woman who endure their husband's kicks."

Udaybhanulal declared, "I earn the money, and I will spend it as I wish. No one has the right to tell me otherwise."

Kalyani said, "Then take care of your own house! I bow out from a house where I have no say. I have just as much right to this home as you do — not an inch less. If you think you are the king of your own, then remember, I am the queen of mine. Keep your house; I have no shortage of food for myself. Your children are yours to treat as you like — love them or destroy them. If I don't see it, it won't hurt me. Out of sight, out of mind!"

Udaybhanulal replied, "Do you really think that if you don't take care of this house, it will fall apart? I can take care of ten houses like this all by myself."

Kalyani retorted, "Oh really? If this house isn't in shambles within a month, then I'll believe what you say!"

As she spoke, Kalyani's face flushed with anger. She stormed up and walked towards the door. Babu Udaybhanulal, who was known for his sharp arguments in court, had little understanding of the emotions of women. It's one subject where even the wisest men remain ignorant. If he had softened now, held Kalyani's hand, and asked her to sit back down, she might have stayed. But instead, he added one more blow as she left.

"Is that your pride in your father's house speaking?"

Kalyani stopped at the door, turned back, her eyes blazing, and said, "My parents are not the ones responsible for my fate, nor am I so low that I would go begging for their bread."

Udaybhanulal asked, "Then where will you go?"

Kalyani replied, "Who are you to ask me that? In God's creation, there is space for countless creatures. Do you think there is no place for me?"

With those words, Kalyani walked out of the room. She stepped into the courtyard and glanced up at the sky, as if calling the stars to witness how heartlessly she was being thrown out of her home. It was eleven o'clock at night, and the house was silent. The two boys' cots were in her room. She went back to her room and saw Chanderbhanu asleep, while the youngest, Suryabhanu, sat up on his cot. Seeing his mother, he said, "Where were you, mother?"

Kalyani, standing a little distance away, replied, "Nowhere, my son. I had gone to see your father."

Suryabhanu said, "You went away, and I was scared all alone. Why did you go, mother? Tell me."

Saying this, the little one stretched out his arms to be picked up. Kalyani could no longer hold herself back. Her heart, parched by anger, was overwhelmed by the soothing flow of maternal love. The tender emotions that had withered in the heat of her rage now blossomed again. Her eyes filled with tears as she picked up the child and held him close. "Why didn't you call out to me, my dear?"

Suryabhanu said, "I did call, but you didn’t listen. Promise you won’t leave again."

Kalyani replied, "No, my love, I won't leave again."

With that, Kalyani lay down on the cot with Suryabhanu in her arms. As soon as he nestled against his mother's heart, the child fell asleep. Kalyani's mind, however, was torn. She remembered her husband's words and felt like leaving the house for good, but when she looked at her children, her heart melted with love. Who would she leave her precious little ones with? Who would take care of them, and who would they belong to? Who would feed them in the morning, put them to sleep, and wake up with them? Her little children would be left with nothing. No, my dear ones, I will not leave you. I will endure everything for you — the insults, the harsh words, the scolding — all of it, for your sake.

Kalyani lay down with the child, but Babu Udaybhanulal could not sleep. Hurtful words are difficult to forget. "What a temperament! As if I am her servant! It's hard to get a word out. Should I just be her slave now? She wants to have the house all to herself, and everyone else should be thrown out. She probably wishes I were dead so she could live comfortably on her own. No matter how much you try to hide it, your true feelings eventually come out. I've been hearing such harsh words from her for days. She must be proud of her father's house, but no one will care for her there. Right now, they are all respectful, but once she actually goes there for help, reality will hit her. She'll leave crying. What arrogance! She thinks she runs this household. If I leave for four days, all her pride will come crashing down. I should break her arrogance once and for all. Let her taste widowhood for a while. How does she even have the courage to curse me like this? It seems love has never touched her, or maybe she thinks I'm so attached to this home that no matter how much she curses me, I won't leave. Well, she's mistaken. I'm not one of those who cling to the world! To hell with this house and the people in it. Is this a home or a hell? A man comes home tired from outside, expecting some peace, but instead, he has to listen to curses. Prayers are being made for my death. Is this the end of twenty-five years of marriage? Fine, I'll leave. Once I see all her arrogance turn to dust and her attitude cooled, I'll return. Four or five days should be enough. Let her remember who she picked a fight with.

With these thoughts, Babu Udaybhanulal got up, draped a silk shawl around his neck, took some money, put his identification card into the pocket of another kurta, picked up his walking staff, and quietly stepped outside. All the servants were fast asleep. The dog, hearing the noise, woke up and followed him.

But who knew that this entire play was being orchestrated by fate? The merciless puppeteer of life's grand stage was sitting in some mysterious place, weaving his intricate and cruel plot. Who could have imagined that the pretense was about to turn into reality, that the performance would take the shape of truth?

Night had conquered the moon, establishing its rule. Its demonic forces had cast their shadow upon nature. Virtue lay hidden, while vice strutted about in arrogant victory. Wild animals roamed the forest in search of prey, and in the cities, human predators prowled the streets.

Babu Udaybhanulal hurried towards the Ganges. He had made up his mind to leave for Mirzapur for five days, leaving his kurta on the riverbank. Seeing his clothes, people would think he had drowned. The identity card was in the pocket of the kurta, so there would be no difficulty in identifying him. Within moments, the entire city would hear the news. By eight in the morning, the entire town would be gathered at my door — then let's see what my dear wife does.

As Babu Udaybhanulal walked through the narrow alleys, he suddenly heard footsteps behind him. He thought it was probably just someone passing by. He quickened his pace, but every time he turned into another lane, the person behind him would turn as well. This made Babu Udaybhanulal suspicious — it seemed like the man was following him. He had an uneasy feeling that the person had ill intentions. He quickly took out his pocket lantern and shone its light on the man. It was an older man, carrying a blackjack on his shoulder. Babu Udaybhanulal was startled upon seeing him. This was a notorious criminal from the city. Three years ago, he had been accused of robbery, and Udaybhanulal had prosecuted him on behalf of the government, resulting in the man's three-year imprisonment. Ever since, he had held a grudge against Udaybhanulal, thirsting for revenge. The man had been released just the day before. And now, by a twist of fate, he had found Babu Udaybhanulal alone at night — a perfect opportunity to settle scores. Such an opportunity might not come again. He had been following Udaybhanulal, waiting for the right moment to strike, but as soon as Babu Udaybhanulal lit the lantern, the man paused and said, "Why, Babuji, do you recognize me? I am Matey."

Babu Udaybhanulal scolded, "Why are you following me?"

Matey responded, "Why? Is it forbidden to walk on the road? Is this lane your father's property?"

Babu Udaybhanulal had wrestled in his youth and was still a strong man. He was not faint-hearted either. Gripping his stick tightly, he said, "Haven't had enough yet, have you? This time, you'll go away for seven years."

Matey replied, "Whether I go away for seven years or fourteen, I won't let you live. But if you fall at my feet and swear that you won't prosecute anyone anymore, I'll spare you. Do you agree?"

Udaybhanulal retorted, "Have you lost your mind?"

Matey grinned, "No, it's your doom that's come. Will you swear — one!"

Udaybhanulal said, "Will you back off, or should I call the policeman?"

Matey continued, "Two!"

Udaybhanulal shouted, "Get out of my way, you scoundrel!"

Matey said, "Three!"

The moment the word 'three' left Matey's mouth, he brought the blackjack down on Babu Udaybhanulal's head with all his strength. Udaybhanulal fell to the ground unconscious, only managing to say, "Oh! He killed me!"

Matey approached to inspect. Babu Udaybhanulal's head was split open, and blood was flowing. There was no sign of a pulse. Matey understood that the job was done. He removed the gold watch from Udaybhanulal's wrist, took the gold buttons from his kurta, pulled the ring from his finger, and walked away as if nothing had happened. But he showed enough mercy to drag the body to the side of the road. Alas, what had he thought would happen, and what had transpired! Life — is there anything more fleeting in this world? Is it not as fragile as a lamp that gets extinguished by a gust of wind? You see a bubble on the water, but even it takes a moment to burst; life doesn't have even that much substance. What is the guarantee of a breath? Yet we build grand palaces of desires on this transience, without knowing whether the breath we exhale will return. And we plan so far ahead as if we are immortal.

# Chapter - 3

*If you seek a tale where flowers bloom untouched by the winds, where words spoken bear no thorns, and hearts are like mirrors unbroken—this is not that story. Here the lines blur between right and wrong, and promises unravel like fading silk. This story is a dance of fragility, a song where the melody trembles and breaks, echoing the truth that not all endings wear the garb of light. Enter gently, and hold not to illusions, for the journey ahead is as raw as the human spirit itself.*

We won't burden the readers with the lamentations of a broken heart or the cries of orphans. Those who suffer, they cry, mourn, and grieve — this is nothing new. However, if you wish, you may try to imagine the immense mental torment Kalyani was enduring, haunted by the thought that she herself was the cause of her beloved's demise. The words that had escaped her mouth in a fit of rage now pierced her heart like arrows. If her husband had breathed his last in her lap, groaning in pain, she would have at least found solace in knowing that she had fulfilled her duty towards him. There is no greater comfort for a grieving heart than knowing that their beloved left the world with love in their heart until the very end. But Kalyani did not have this comfort. She thought, 'Alas! My twenty-five years of devotion have gone in vain. In his final moments, I was deprived of my husband's love. If only I hadn't spoken such harsh words, he would never have left the house that night.' She wondered what thoughts must have crossed his mind. Imagining his emotions and magnifying her guilt, she spent every waking moment in agony. The children she once cherished now became a source of annoyance to her. 'It was because of them that I quarrelled with my husband. They are my enemies,' she thought.

Where once there was constant activity, filled with relatives and laughter, now there was only emptiness. The lively gatherings had vanished. When the provider was no longer there, the dependents could not stay. Gradually, within a month, all the nephews and other relatives left. Those who once swore loyalty and claimed they would spill their blood for the family ran away without even looking back. The world seemed completely changed. The children she once wanted to hold close now appeared lifeless, their faces dull, and flies buzzed around them. Where had their youthful glow gone?

As the waves of grief subsided, the issue of Nirmala's marriage resurfaced. Some suggested postponing the wedding for the year, but Kalyani firmly opposed this idea. She said, 'After all the preparations, canceling the wedding would mean all our efforts would go to waste, and we would have to repeat everything next year, which seems unlikely. It is better to proceed with the wedding now. There is no dowry involved, and the arrangements for the guests are already made. Delaying it will only lead to more losses.' Thus, a message was sent to Mahashay Bhalchandra, along with an expression of regret for the current circumstances.

In her letter, Kalyani wrote, 'Please have mercy on this helpless woman and help a sinking boat reach the shore. My husband had many dreams and hopes, but fate had other plans. Now, my honor lies in your hands. The girl is already yours. I consider it my good fortune to serve your guests, but if there are any shortcomings or mistakes, please be compassionate, considering my current situation. I trust that you will not let this orphan be subject to blame.

Kalyani did not send this letter by post but instead asked the family priest, Purohit Motiram, 'It may be an inconvenience, but could you personally deliver this letter for me? And please, convey my humble request that the fewer people who attend, the better. There is no one here to handle all the arrangements.'

Purohit Motiram took the letter and arrived in Lucknow on the third day.

It was evening. Babu Bhalchandra lay sprawled on an armchair in front of the drawing-room, smoking a hookah. He was an extremely large, tall man, looking almost like a dark deity or perhaps a captured African giant. From head to toe, his complexion was dark — so dark that it was impossible to tell where his forehead ended and his hair began. He looked like a living statue of coal. The summer heat was particularly unbearable for him; two servants stood fanning him, yet beads of sweat formed continuously on his forehead. Babu Bhalchandra held a high position in the excise department, earning a salary of five hundred rupees a month. He took hefty bribes from contractors. Whether the contractors sold diluted liquor or kept their shops open twenty-four hours, all that mattered was keeping him happy. The law, in his eyes, was only as strict as his satisfaction. His appearance was so fearsome that people would startle at the sight of him, even on a moonlit night — not just children and women, but grown men too. The reason for mentioning a moonlit night is that, on a dark night, he could hardly be seen at all — his dark complexion blended completely into the darkness. The only color visible were his red eyes. Just as a devout Muslim prays five times a day, Babu Bhalchandra drank alcohol five times daily. Being in charge of alcohol, he could drink as much as he wanted without anyone questioning him. Whenever he felt thirsty, he drank. Just as some colors complement each other, some oppose each other — the redness of his eyes made his darkness even more menacing.

As soon as Babu Bhalchandra saw Purohitji, he rose from his chair and exclaimed, 'Ah, it's you? Come, come! What an honor!' He called out, 'Is anyone there? Where have they all gone? Jhagdu, Gurdin, Chhakori, Bhawani, Ramgulam, anyone? Have they all died? Hurry, Ramgulam, Bhawani, Chhakori, Gurdin, Jhagdu! No one responds, they're all dead! There are a dozen people here, but when it's time to work, not a single one is around. Who knows where they all vanish to. Bring a chair for our guest!'

Babu Bhalchandra repeated the five names several times, but it never occurred to him to send one of the men fanning him to fetch a chair. A few minutes later, a one-eyed servant approached, coughing, and said,

'Sir, I can't keep doing this work. I've grown tired of running here and there, borrowing things and asking for favors.'

Bhalchandra snapped, 'Stop whining and go get a chair. Whenever you're asked to do something, you start complaining.' He then turned to Purohitji and said, 'Tell me, Purohitji, how is everything there?'

Motiram replied, 'What can I say, Babuji, things are far from well. The entire household is in ruins.'

Just then, the servant brought a broken pine box and set it down, saying, 'I can't carry any more chairs or tables.'

Purohitji, feeling embarrassed, sat down on it cautiously, fearing it might break, and handed Kalyani's letter to Babu Bhalchandra.

Bhalchandra read the letter, his face turning somber. He sighed heavily and said, 'How much more will be ruined now? What greater misfortune can fall upon us? Babu Udaybhanu Lal was an old friend of mine. He wasn't just a man, he was a gem! What a heart he had, what courage!' He paused, wiping his eyes, and continued, 'It's as if I've lost my right hand. Believe me, ever since I heard the news, it feels like darkness has enveloped my eyes. I sit down to eat, but can't swallow a bite. His face stands before my eyes, and I leave the meal unfinished. I can't focus on anything. Even the grief of losing a brother feels less painful than this. He wasn't just a man, he was a gem!'

Motiram added, 'There is no nobleman like him left in the town now, sir.'

Bhalchandra nodded, 'I know well, Purohitji. What can you tell me that I don't know? Such a person is one in a million. No one else knew him as well as I did. After only two or three meetings, I became devoted to him, and that devotion will last until my dying breath. Please tell Mrs. Udaybhanu that I feel a deep sorrow in my heart.'

Motiram added, 'I expected nothing less from you, Babuji. Today, the sight of gentlemen like you is rare. Otherwise, who would marry their son without a dowry these days?'

Bhalchandra responded, 'Panditji, dowry is not something you discuss with a man of integrity like Udaybhanu Lal. Just being related to him is worth a million rupees to me. I consider it my great fortune. Ah, what a generous soul he was. Money meant nothing to him, not even as much as a straw. The custom of dowry is terrible, absolutely terrible! If I had my way, I would shoot both those who demand dowry and those who give it — yes, sir, I would shoot them on the spot, even if it meant facing the gallows! Ask them, are you marrying off your son, or are you selling him? If you want to spend lavishly on your son's wedding, do so by all means, but do it with your own money. Why slit the throat of the girl's father? It's vile, utterly vile! If I had my way, I would shoot these scoundrels.'

Motiram said, 'Bless you, sir! God has given you great wisdom. This is the grace of righteousness. The mistress wishes for the wedding to proceed as planned, and she has written everything in the letter. Now, it is only you who can save us. We will, of course, serve all the guests who attend, but the situation has changed drastically, sir. There is no one to manage everything. Please, make sure that nothing tarnishes the name of Babu Udaybhanu Lal.'

Bhalchandra closed his eyes for a minute, then sighed deeply and said, 'It wasn't meant to be that Lakshmi would enter my home; otherwise, why would this calamity have struck? All my hopes are now in ruins. I was overjoyed that the auspicious time was near, but who knew that fate had another plot in store? Just the memory of my late friend is enough to make me weep. Seeing the girl would only deepen the wound. In that state, who knows what I might do? Call it a virtue or a fault, but once I form a bond, it stays etched in my heart. Right now, his image keeps haunting me, but if the girl were to come into my home, I wouldn't be able to go on living. Believe me, I would cry my eyes out. I know well that weeping and lamenting are in vain. The dead do not return. We must resign ourselves to patience, but my heart is not in my control. Seeing that orphan girl would tear me apart.'

Motiram said, 'Please don't say this, sir! If Babu Udaybhanu Lal is no more, then you are there. You are now like her father. She is no longer just his daughter; she is yours too. People will not understand your heartfelt emotions; they will think that you broke your promise because of his death. This would bring you disrepute. Please, calm your heart and conduct the marriage with joy. Even though a great calamity has struck, the mistress will leave no stone unturned in serving and respecting your family and guests.'

Babu Bhalchandra realized that Purohit Motiram was not just a scholar of scriptures but also adept in practical matters. He said, 'Panditji, I swear that I love that girl more than my own daughter, but what power do I have when fate has other plans? His death is an ominous sign sent by the Almighty. It's a warning of an impending disaster, a message from the heavens that this marriage will not be auspicious. In such a situation, think yourself, how appropriate would this union be? You are a learned man; consider this — when something begins with misfortune, how can it end well? One does not knowingly swallow a fly. Please explain this to Mrs. Udaybhanu. I am ready to follow her wishes, but the outcome will not be favorable. As one who holds his interests dear, I cannot allow such an injustice to my dear friend's child.'

This argument left Purohit Motiram speechless. The plaintiff had fired an arrow for which the defendant had no defense. His opponent had used his own weapon against him, and he had no way to counter it. He was still thinking of a response when Babu Bhalchandra once again started calling out for his servants, 'Oh, you've all disappeared again — Jhagdu, Chhakori, Bhawani, Gurudin, Ramgulam! Not one of you responds; have you all died? Has anyone thought of getting some water for Panditji? Who knows how to make these people understand anything. They seem to lack any sense. They can see that a respectable guest has come from afar, exhausted, yet no one cares. Bring some water at least. Panditji, should I prepare a sherbet for you, or perhaps order some sweets for you?'

Motiram would accept no limitations when it came to sweets. His philosophy was that anything prepared in ghee became inherently pure. Rasgullas and besan laddus were his favorites, but sherbet did not interest him in the least. Filling his stomach with mere water was against his principles. Hesitating slightly, he said, "I am not accustomed to drinking sherbet, but I can certainly have some sweets."

Bhalchandra: Fruit-based, right?

Motiram: I have no such considerations.

Bhalchandra: Exactly. All this fuss about caste and purity is mere nonsense. I don't believe in it at all. Hey, has no one arrived yet? Chhakodi, Bhavani, Gurudeen, Ramgulam, anyone?

Again, the same old servant came forward, coughing, and stood before him, saying, "Sir, please give me my salary and let me go. I cannot handle this kind of work anymore. Running here and there makes my legs ache."

Bhalchandra: Whether you work or not, you always want your salary first! You spend the entire day coughing, yet your pay keeps accumulating. Now go to the market and bring fresh sweets worth a rupee. Off you go, quickly!

After giving these orders to the servant, Bhalchandra went inside the house and addressed his wife, "A Priest has arrived from there. He has brought a letter. Please read it."

His wife's name was Rangilibai. She was a fair-skinned, cheerful woman. Though beauty and youth were slowly departing from her, like dear friends, they clung to her for thirty years, unwilling to part so easily.

Rangilibai was seated, preparing paan. She responded, "I have already told you, I do not wish to agree to that marriage."

Bhalchandra: Yes, I conveyed that, but I couldn't get the words out without some hesitation. I had to create an excuse.

Rangili: Why hesitate to speak clearly? We don't wish to go through with it, and we haven't taken anything from anyone. If we're getting ten thousand in cash from somewhere else, why shouldn't we go there? Their daughter isn't made of gold. If the lawyer were alive, he would've given fifteen or twenty thousand reluctantly. Now, what's left there?

Bhalchandra: It's not right to go back on our word once given. No one might say anything openly, but our reputation will suffer. However, I'm forced by your stubbornness.

Rangili took a betel leaf, chewed it, and then opened the letter. Bhalchandra had no familiarity with Hindi at all, and though Rangili rarely read any books, she could manage to read letters. As she read the first line, her eyes moistened, and by the time she finished, tears were streaming down her face—each word was steeped in compassion, and every letter dripped with humility. Rangili's hardness wasn't like stone, but rather like wax that melts with a single touch of warmth. Kalyani's poignant words melted her self-centered heart. With a choked voice, she asked, "Is the priest still here?"

Seeing his wife's tears, Bhalchandra felt drained. He regretted showing her the letter. What was the need for it? Never had he made such a mistake before. With uncertainty, he replied, "He might be. I told him to leave, though."

Rangili peeked out of the window. Pandit Motiram was sitting like a crane, watching the road leading to the market. He restlessly shifted from one side to the other. The "one-rupee sweets" had already shattered his hope, and now the delay made his situation even more pitiful. Seeing him still seated there, Rangili said, "Oh! He's still here.

Go and tell him—we will go through with the marriage, certainly. The poor woman is in such trouble."

Bhalchandra: Sometimes you talk like a child. I've just told him that I'm not willing to go through with the marriage. I had to give a long and elaborate explanation. Now if I go and give the opposite message, what will he think of me? Just think about it. This isn't a child's game, where you decide one thing and then immediately change it. A gentleman's word cannot be treated like a joke.

Rangili: Fine, don't say it yourself. Send the priest to me. I will explain it in a way that both your words and mine remain intact. Surely, you have no objection to that?

Bhalchandra: You think everyone in the world, except yourself, is naive. Whether you say it or I say it, it's the same. What is decided is decided; I won't bring it up again. You were the one insisting that I shouldn't go ahead with it, which led me to retract my word. Now you're changing your mind again. This is like grinding lentils on my chest. Don't you care about my dignity at all?

Rangili: How was I to know that a widow's situation had become so miserable? You were the one who said she had hidden her husband's entire fortune and was pretending to be poor to gain sympathy. A cunning woman, you said. I believed what you told me. There's shame and hesitation in doing wrong after doing good, but there's no hesitation in doing good after doing wrong. If you had agreed and I said no afterward, then your hesitation would be justified. But agreeing after refusing—that's nobility.

Bhalchandra: You might consider it nobility, but to me, it feels like deceit. And how did you decide that what I said about the lawyer's wife was false? Was it by reading that letter? Just because you're straightforward, you think everyone else is as well.

Rangili: There doesn't seem to be any pretense in this letter. A fabricated story doesn't touch the heart the way this did.

Bhalchandra: Sometimes a lie is so well-crafted that the truth seems pale in comparison. Those storytellers whose books make you cry for hours, do you think they write the truth? They weave pure fabrications—it's an art.

Rangili: Are you mocking me? Are you trying to hide things from me like a patient hides things from his Doctor? When I accept your words, you think you've fooled me. But I know every inch of you. You try to pin your flaws on me to make yourself look spotless. Tell me, am I saying anything false? When the lawyer was alive, you thought there was no need to make demands; he'd give what he found appropriate, and more without any insistence. Now that he's gone, you've started making all sorts of excuses. This isn't gentlemanly—it's petty. And it's your fault. I won't go near this marriage anymore. Do whatever you want. I detest hypocrites. Whatever you do, be transparent—good or bad. This "one face for the world, another in reality" doesn't suit you. So, tell me, are you going ahead with the marriage or not?

Bhalchandra: Since I'm deceitful, dishonest, and a liar, why ask me anything? But oh, how well you understand people! Really, you deserve praise.

Rangili: Yes, go on. Such a righteous man, yet you feel no shame. Honestly, did I not see through everything?

Bhalchandra: Alright, fine. Some women can truly understand men. I used to think that women had sharp intuition, but today I've lost that belief. Now I have to accept what sages have said about women.

Rangili: Just go look in the mirror. I swear by me—see how embarrassed you look.

Bhalchandra: Tell me honestly, how embarrassed do I look?

Rangili: Just as much as a decent person caught in a theft would look.

Bhalchandra: Alright, alright, I admit it. But the marriage will still not happen.

Rangili: Fine, do as you wish. Why don't you ask Bhuvan once?

Bhalchandra: Very well, let him decide.

Rangili: Not even a hint from you!

Bhalchandra: I won't even look his way.

As luck would have it, Bhuvanmohan arrived at that very moment. Such handsome, well-built young men are rarely seen in colleges. He took after his mother—fair-skinned, lips as delicate as rose petals, broad forehead, large eyes; but his physique was like his father's—tall and robust. A high-collared coat, breeches, tie, boots, and hat suited him perfectly. He carried a hockey stick, walked with the confidence of youth, and had a sense of self-pride in his eyes.

Rangili said, "You took quite a long time today, didn't you? Look at this, a letter has come from your in-laws. Your mother-in-law has written it. Tell me clearly now, do you want to marry there or not?"

Bhuvan replied, "I should marry, mother, but I won't."

Rangili asked, "Why not?"

Bhuvan said, "Marry me into a family that can offer a substantial amount of money. If not a lot, at least a lakh should be guaranteed. What's left there now? The Lawyer is no more, and what could the old lady possibly have left?"

Rangili frowned, "Aren't you ashamed to say things like this?"

Bhuvan responded, "What's there to be ashamed of? Who hates money? A lakh of rupees is something I can't save in a lifetime. Even if I pass this year, it will take at least five years before I see any money. Then, I might start earning a mere hundred or two hundred rupees a month. By the time I reach five or six hundred, most of my life will be gone. There will be no chance to save anything significant. If I could marry a wealthy girl, life would be comfortable."

Rangili shot back, "No matter what kind of girl she is?"

Bhuvan said, "Wealth hides all flaws. Even if she insults me, I wouldn't complain. Who minds the kick of a cow that gives milk?"

Bhalchandra, in a tone of agreement, said, "We sympathize with those people and are saddened that God has put them in such distress, but decisions must be made wisely. No matter how poor we are, a decent wedding will still take place. But over there, even food isn't guaranteed. The only result will be people laughing at us."

Rangili, with scorn, said, "You two, father and son, are truly two peas in a pod. Both of you are ready to cut that poor girl's throat."

Bhuvan, defensively, said, "The poor should make relations with those who are like them. Going beyond one's means..."

Rangili interrupted, "Oh, stop it. Who do you think you are? A great millionaire? If someone knocks at your door, they'd be lucky to get even a glass of water from you! And you talk about wealth!"

With that, Rangili stood up and went to arrange the kitchen.

Bhuvanmohan, smiling, went to his room, while Bhalchandra twisted his moustache and stepped out, intending to inform Motiram of his final decision. But Motiram was nowhere to be found.

Motiram had waited for the servant for a while, but when he took too long, he couldn't sit idle any longer. He thought to himself that simply waiting here wouldn't solve anything—he needed to do something. Relying on fate alone, he'd surely starve here. He stealthily picked up his stick and headed in the direction the servant had gone. The market was nearby; he reached there in no time. He found the old man sitting at a sweet shop, smoking his hookah. Seeing him, Motiram said casually, "Is nothing ready yet, my friend? The master is sitting there, fuming, wondering if you went off to sleep or are drinking toddy. I told him, 'Sir, that's not the case. The old man is slow; he'll be back as soon as he can.' Such peculiar people, I must say. I don't know how they keep servants."

The servant replied, "No one else has lasted here except me, and no one else will. I haven't been paid for a year. He don't pay anyone. If anyone asks for wages, he start scolding. The poor fellow leaves the job. Those two men who were fanning him are government servants. They've been assigned by the authorities, which is why they're here. I keep thinking, 'Let it go on as it is.' This year has passed, maybe another year or two will also pass."

Motiram asked, "So you're the only one left? They call out the names of so many servants."

The servant laughed, "All those names belong to people who came and left within the last two or three months. They keep repeating their names to show off. Can you help me find another job?"

Motiram reassured him, "Oh, there are plenty of jobs. It's hard to find good servants these days. You're experienced; finding a job won't be a problem for you. Now, anything fresh here? He was asking me if I'd have khichdi or bati. I said, 'Sir, he's an old man, and it'd be hard for him to cook at night. I'll just eat something from the market.' He said, 'Alright, you'll find the servant at the shop.' Tell me, shopkeeper, do you have anything fresh? The laddus look good—give me about a kilo. Should I come up there to eat?"

Saying this, Motiram sat down at the sweet shop and began sampling the delicacies. He ate heartily—devouring around two to three kilos. As he ate, he praised the shopkeeper, "Oh, shopkeeper, your reputation precedes you, and your sweets live up to it. Those sweet makers in Banaras can't make rasgullas like these. Their kalakand is good, but yours is no less. It's not just about ingredients—it takes skill."

The shopkeeper, flattered, said, "Have some more, Maharaj! Please accept a little rabri from me."

Motiram, pretending reluctance, said, "I don't really feel like it, but give me about a quarter kilo."

The shopkeeper insisted, "Why just a quarter? It's good—take at least half a kilo."

After a fully satisfying meal, Motiram wandered around the market for a while and returned to the house by nine o'clock. The place was quiet, with only a lantern burning. He made his bed on the veranda and went to sleep.

As usual, he woke up around eight in the morning and saw Bhalchandra strolling. Noticing him awake, Bhalchandra bowed and said, " Purohitji, where did you disappear last night? I waited up for you until quite late. All the food was kept ready for so long, but when you didn't come, we put it away. Did you eat anything?"

Motiram replied, "I had some food at the sweet shop."

Bhalchandra, trying to appear generous, said, "Ah, but the pleasure of eating bati and dal can't be compared to just sweets. You must have spent two to three rupees, and yet you wouldn't have been satisfied. You're my guest—please take whatever amount you spent."

Motiram responded, "I ate at your sweet shop, the one at the corner."

Bhalchandra asked, "How much did you have to pay?"

Motiram casually said, "I've put it on your tab."

Bhalchandra said, "Just let me know how many sweets you took, or else he might try to cheat later. He's quite the swindler."

Motiram replied, "It was around two and a half kilos of sweets and half a kilo of rabri."

Bhalchandra's eyes widened in disbelief, as if he had heard something astonishing. Three kilos of sweets—a quantity that wouldn't even be consumed here in an entire month—and this man devoured nearly fifty rupees' worth in one sitting! If he stayed for another day or two, the entire household would be brought to its knees. Was his stomach a bottomless pit? Three kilos—could it be true? Distressed, he rushed inside and said to Rangili, "Do you hear me? This fellow polished off three kilos of sweets yesterday. Three whole kilos!"

Rangili, astonished, said, "No way! How could anyone eat three kilos? Is he a man or a bull?"

Bhalchandra said, "He himself claims three kilos. It must be at least four—he's not going to understate it."

Rangili said sarcastically, "Is there a demon inside his belly or what?"

Bhalchandra added, "If he stays today, he'll aim for six kilos."

Rangili, exasperated, said, "Then why let him stay today at all? Just give him the reply to the letter and send him off. If he insists on staying, tell him clearly that sweets aren't free here. He can cook khichdi if he likes, or else leave. Those who find pleasure in feeding such gluttons can do so—we certainly do not!"

But the priest was ready to depart, so Bhalchandra didn't need to use much tact.

He asked, "Are you prepared, Purohitji?"

Motiram: "Yes, sir. I am ready to leave now. The nine o'clock train will do, right?"

Bhalchandra: "Why not stay a bit longer today?"

Even as he said this, Bhalchandra feared that the Purohitji might actually decide to stay, so he hastily added, "Yes, well, they must be waiting for you there too."

Motiram: "Staying a day or two wouldn't have mattered, and I did think of taking a dip in Triveni. But, if you don't mind me saying so, you people have not an ounce of respect for Brahmins. Our patrons, they eagerly await our orders, eager to fulfill them. When we reach them, they consider it their good fortune, and the entire household, from the youngest to the oldest, is absorbed in serving us. Where there's no respect, it's intolerable to stay even a moment. Where there's no respect for a Brahmin, prosperity cannot exist."

Bhalchandra: "Purohitji, we haven't wronged you in any way."

Motiram: "No wrongdoing? And what do you call wrongdoing then? Just now, you went inside and said that this gentleman devoured three kilos of sweets. Have you even seen those who really know how to eat? Feed them once, and your eyes will open wide. Great men exist who can eat half a maund of sweets without even a burp. People plead with us to eat a sweet, pay us for it. We are not begging

Brahmins who linger at your door. I heard of your name and came here, unaware that I would struggle even for a meal. Go on, may God bless you!"

Bhalchandra was so embarrassed that he couldn't utter a word. In his entire life, he had never been scolded like that. He made many excuses, claiming that it wasn't about him, but about someone else entirely. Still, Purohitji's anger wouldn't subside. He could endure anything but an insult to his appetite. Just as a woman's beauty is sensitive to criticism, a man's pride can be hurt by criticism of his appetite. Bhalchandra tried to pacify him, but he feared that Purohitji might stay. His stinginess had been exposed; that much was clear. Covering that up was now essential. To hide his miserliness, Bhalchandra left no stone unturned, but what was destined had happened. He regretted ever talking about it inside the house and, even more, saying it aloud. The rascal had listened in, and there was no undoing it now. Who knew what ill omen had befallen that led to this misfortune! If Purohitji left upset, he would spread rumors and ruin Bhalchandra's entire reputation. His mouth had to be shut.

With that thought, he went back inside and said to Rangili Bai, "This rascal heard every word of our conversation. He's leaving in a huff."

Rangili: "If you knew he was at the door, why didn't you speak softly?"

Bhalchandra: "Misfortune doesn't come alone. How could I have known he was eavesdropping outside?"

Rangili: "Who knows what ill omen brought this on?"

Bhalchandra: "He was lying right there. If I knew, I wouldn't have even looked in that direction. Now, we need to give him something to pacify him."

Rangili: "Oh, let it go. If you're not going through with the marriage, why do you care? Let him think what he wants, let him say what he wants."

Bhalchandra: "That's no way to get through this. Here, let me give him hundred rupees as a farewell gift. May God never bring his wretched face before us again."

Reluctantly, Rangili handed over hundred rupees, and Bhalchandra took them to Purohitji, placing them at his feet. Purohitji thought to himself, "You miser! You think you can silence me with hundred rupees? Don't be mistaken; I know every vein of yours." He pocketed the money and blessed Bhalchandra before heading on his way.

Bhalchandra stood for a long time, wondering, "I don't know if he still thinks I'm a miser or if the matter is settled. Have these rupees been wasted?"

# Chapter - 4

*If you have come here looking for love's triumph or the glitter of a fortunate alliance, you may be sorely disappointed. The story that unfolds in these pages is not one of fairytale endings or glorious unions. It is a story of compromises, of sacrifices, of a mother weighed down by the burden of her daughter's future, and the harsh realities of widowhood. Here, expectations crumble and dreams turn into mere negotiations. But within this struggle, there lies resilience—the resilience of a mother fighting against fate itself, seeking a sliver of hope amidst despair. If you wish to witness love in its rawest, most sacrificial form, then step into this story. But if happy endings are what you crave, I must ask you to turn away now.*

A heavy storm now gathered over Kalyani's head. It was the first true taste of hardship she had since her husband passed away. What fate could be harsher for a poor widow than having an unmarried daughter? Boys could run around barefoot, chores could be managed somehow, and life could be made to move forward even in a tattered home. But a young daughter, blooming and growing, could not be left waiting forever. Kalyani's heart raged against Bhalchandra. She felt like shaming him publicly, tearing out his hair, shouting that he was not worthy of his father's name. Purohit Motiram had laid bare every last detail of Bhalchandra's deceit.

As she sat there, anger seething inside her, Krishna came in while playing and asked innocently, "Mother, when will the wedding procession arrive? The priest has already come back."

Kalyani: "Are you dreaming of the wedding procession?"

Krishna: "Chander said the wedding procession will come in two or three days. Won't it come, Mother?"

Kalyani: "I've already told you once. Stop pestering me."

Krishna: "Everyone else has a wedding coming to their homes. Why doesn't it come to ours?"

Kalyani: "The one who was supposed to bring the wedding to our home has set his own house on fire."

Krishna, puzzled: "Really, Mother? Then the whole house must have burned down. Where will they live now? Where will sister go?"

Kalyani sighed: "Oh, silly child, you don't understand. There was no real fire. He just decided not to marry here."

Krishna: "But why, Mother? Wasn't everything already settled?"

Kalyani: "He wants more money. I have nothing to give him."

Krishna: "He's really that greedy, Mother?"

Kalyani: "If he's not greedy, then what is he? He's a butcher—merciless and deceitful."

Krishna: "Then it's good that sister isn't marrying into their family. How would she have lived there? This is something to be happy about, Mother. Why are you so sad?"

Kalyani looked at her daughter with love. How true her innocent words were! They cut straight to the heart of the matter. Indeed, this was something to rejoice in—there was no reason to be sad over a broken tie with someone so unworthy. What fate would poor Nirmala have faced with such people? She would have wept her whole life. If even a bit more ghee went into the lentils, the whole household would have screamed; if the food was slightly overcooked, her mother-in-law would have made it into a storm. The boy was greedy too. It was truly a blessing that the marriage did not happen. Otherwise, Nirmala would have cried all her days. As Kalyani rose from her place, her heart felt lighter.

But the marriage still had to be arranged, preferably within the year; otherwise, next year everything would have to be prepared again from scratch. She no longer hoped for a perfect match, nor a wealthy home. What hope did an unfortunate widow like her have for an ideal son-in-law or family? Now she only wanted to lift the burden from her shoulders—any way to secure her daughter's future, even if it meant casting her into the dark unknown. Let her beauty, her grace, her talents mean whatever they might. Without a dowry, none of it mattered. With a dowry, any flaw would be overlooked. A person's worth didn't matter; only the dowry did. What a twisted game of fate!

Kalyani herself was not entirely without fault. Just because she was weak and widowed did not mean she had no shortcomings. She loved her sons more than her daughters. Sons were the oxen who pulled the family's plow; they deserved the first share of the fodder, and whatever remained went to the cows. She had a house, some savings, and jewelry worth a few thousand rupees, but she also had to raise her two sons and educate them. Another daughter would also need to be married in four or five years. She couldn't afford a large dowry for Nirmala, for she had her sons to think of too. Would they not wonder if they ever had a father?

It had been fifteen days since Purohit Motiram returned from Lucknow. He had begun his search for a groom the very next day. He had vowed to show the people in Lucknow that they were not the only ones in the world—there were many more like them. Each day, Kalyani counted the days. Today, she decided to write him a letter. She had just sat down with her pen and ink when Purohit Motiram arrived.

Kalyani: "Ah, Panditji, please come in. I was just about to write to you. When did you return?"

Motiram: "I returned this morning, but I received an invitation from a wealthy patron right away. It had been many days since I'd tasted any delicacies, so I thought I'd deal with that first. I've just returned from there—they were serving about five hundred Brahmins."

Kalyani: "Did anything come of it, or was it just another wasted journey?"

Motiram: "Why would it be a waste? How could it be? I've spoken at five different places. I have the details of all five—pick whichever you prefer. Look, this boy's father is a postal clerk, earning a hundred rupees a month. The boy is still studying, but he has good prospects. There is no property in the family, but the boy seems promising. They belong to a good lineage, and they are asking for three thousand rupees, though I think they will settle for two."

Kalyani: "Does the boy have any brothers?"

Motiram: "No, but he has three unmarried sisters. The mother is still alive. Now, let's move on to the next one. This boy works for the railway, earning fifty rupees a month. He's an orphan—both parents are gone. He's very handsome, well-behaved, and healthy. But the family background isn't great—some say his mother was a barber's wife, others say she was a Thakur's widow. His father worked as a clerk for a princely state. There is some property, but it's burdened with a few thousand rupees of debt. No dowry is needed here. He's around twenty years old."

Kalyani: "If it weren't for the family background, I would agree. One cannot knowingly swallow a fly."

Motiram: "Here's the third one. A landlord's son, with an income of around a thousand rupees a year. They have some farmland too. The boy isn't very educated but knows his way around the courts. He's a widower; his first wife passed away two years ago. They had no children, but the household is large and busy."

Kalyani: "Are they asking for a dowry?"

Motiram: "Don't even ask—four thousand rupees. Now here's the fourth one. The boy is a lawyer, around thirty-five years old. His income is three to four hundred rupees a month. He was married before and has three children. He has built his own house and acquired some property. There's no question of dowry here."

Kalyani: "What's the family background like?"

Motiram: "Very respectable—an old, noble family. Finally, here's the fifth one. The father runs a printing press. The boy studied up to his B.A. but now works in the family business. He's eighteen years old. Apart from the press, they don't have any other property, but they're debt-free. The family isn't very good, but it isn't bad either. The boy is very handsome and well-mannered. They won't agree for less than a thousand rupees, though they're asking for three."

Kalyani: "Which one do you prefer?"

Motiram: "I prefer two—the one from the railway and the one who works at the printing press."

Kalyani: "But didn't you say the railway boy's family has a flaw?"

Motiram: "Yes, that's true. Perhaps the boy from the printing press would be best."

Kalyani: "But where will I get a thousand rupees from? And that's just your guess—they might ask for even more. You can see how things are here—we're lucky to have food on our plates. Where would I get the money? The landlord wants four thousand, and the postal clerk asks for two. Let's forget those. The lawyer seems the only feasible choice. Thirty-five isn't that old. Why not settle on him?"

Motiram: "Think it over thoroughly. I am here to follow your wishes. Wherever you say, I'll finalize it. But don't underestimate the boy from the printing press—he is a gem. With him, your daughter will have a successful life. Just as she is beautiful and talented, he is equally handsome and virtuous."

Kalyani: "I also like him, Panditji, but where will the money come from? Who will give it to me? Is there a benefactor out there? Those who once ate here have now vanished, and they even hold it against me, thinking I pushed them away. Why should I stretch my hand for something beyond my control? Who doesn't love their children? Who doesn't want them to be happy? But only when it's within one's means. Please, Panditji, proceed with arranging the lawyer's proposal. He may be older, but life and death are in God's hands. Thirty-five isn't an age that makes him an old man. If Nirmala is destined for happiness, she will find it wherever she goes. And if sorrow is her fate, then that, too, she will endure. Our Nirmala loves children; she will treat his children as her own. Please find an auspicious time and proceed with the arrangements.

## Chapter - 5

*If you think life settles into happy harmony after marriage, you may wish to reconsider before diving into this story. For Nirmala, the journey has just begun, and it is neither simple nor sweet. What lies ahead is not the fairy-tale romance we are accustomed to, but the struggle of a young bride trying to find meaning and connection in a relationship forged by obligation and social expectation. Dive in, if you dare, but be ready for the rawness of real emotions and unfulfilled desires.*

Nirmala's marriage was completed, and she moved to her in-laws' house. Her husband, Munshi Totaram, was a lawyer. Totaram was a stout, middle-aged man, around forty years of age. Though he was not very old, the strenuous demands of his law practice had left his hair prematurely gray. He had little time for exercise, barely any time for leisure, and as a result, he had grown a noticeable belly. Despite his substantial physique, he was often plagued by ailments—particularly indigestion and hemorrhoids. Thus, he was careful about every step he took.

Totaram had three sons. The eldest, Mansaram, was sixteen years old; the middle one, Jiyaram, was twelve, and the youngest, Siyaram, was seven. All three boys attended English schools. In the house, there was no one else apart from Totaram's widowed sister, Rukmini, who served as the lady of the house. Rukmini was over fifty years old and had no family of her own. She lived permanently at Totaram's place.

Totaram, well-versed in the dynamics of married life, was eager to keep Nirmala happy, filling the gap that naturally existed between them with gifts and tokens of affection. Although he was a miserly man by nature, he would always bring some small present for Nirmala. On important occasions, he did not hesitate to spend money. While only a limited amount of milk was bought for the children, there was no shortage of nuts, sweets, and preserves for Nirmala. Though Totaram had never been fond of entertainment himself, he began taking Nirmala to see films, circuses, and theater performances during holidays. He even spent some of his precious time playing the gramophone with her.

But Nirmala, for reasons she could not quite name, found it difficult to sit close to Totaram or to speak freely with him. Perhaps it was because, until now, the only man of his age she had known was her father—before whom she would bow her head and try to keep herself unnoticed. Now a man of similar age was her husband. She regarded him not as an object of love but as one of respect. She ran from him, her natural cheer vanishing the moment she saw him. Totaram thinks that young women need romance; they need their hearts to be touched and shared openly—only then can they be won over.

Therefore, Totaram left no stone unturned in displaying his affection. Yet, Nirmala found his affection unpleasant. The very words which, coming from a young man's lips, might have filled her heart with joy, sounded hollow, like arrows hitting her heart when spoken by Totaram. They were devoid of excitement, passion, spontaneity, and heart—mere words dressed up in deceit and artificiality. Nirmala did not dislike the perfumes, the fancy clothes, or the outings; what she disliked was sitting beside Totaram. She did not wish to reveal her beauty or youth to him because she felt he had no eyes to truly see them. She did not consider him worthy of enjoying her charms. Just as a delicate flower only blooms in the touch of a morning breeze—Nirmala lacked that gentle breeze in her life.

After the first month of marriage, Totaram made Nirmala the keeper of the household accounts. He would come home from the courts and hand over all the day's earnings to her. He thought Nirmala would be thrilled to see so much money. Nirmala accepted this responsibility with enthusiasm, carefully keeping accounts and noting every penny. If the day's earnings were less than usual, she would even inquire why. She enjoyed talking to Totaram about household matters, and she found these conversations appropriate. But whenever he tried to make a joke or share something light-hearted, her face would turn serious.

When Nirmala adorned herself with clothes and jewelry and saw her reflection in the mirror, her heart would fill with a longing, an unfulfilled desire. A fire seemed to rise in her. She wished she could set the entire house on fire. She blamed her mother for her situation, but her greatest anger was directed at innocent Totaram. She was like a skilled rider forced to mount a lame mule when all she wanted was to ride free. She longed to soar, to experience the ecstatic, lightning-fast pace of passion—but what hope was there in riding a plodding mule?

Perhaps spending time with the children could have helped her forget her condition, at least for a while, brightened her mood. But Rukmini would not even let the children go near her, as if Nirmala was some monster that might devour them. Rukmini's behavior was unpredictable—there was no way to know what would please or upset her. One day, a certain action might make her happy, and the next day, the same action would infuriate her. If Nirmala sat quietly in her room, Rukmini would complain that she brought ill fortune. If Nirmala went to the terrace or chatted with the maids, Rukmini would beat her chest, lamenting that she had no shame and would soon disgrace the family by dancing in the marketplace.

After Totaram handed over the household funds to Nirmala, Rukmini began openly criticizing her. She felt that the end of the world was near. The children often needed small amounts of money. When Rukmini had control, she would manage to get by without giving them any. Now, she sent them straight to Nirmala. Nirmala disliked the children's constant pestering and sometimes refused them. This gave Rukmini a chance to unleash her verbal arrows—"Now she's the mistress of the house. What use are the boys to her? Without a mother, who cares about children? They used to eat sweets paid for by bundles of money, and now they can't even get a penny!"

If Nirmala gave them money without asking questions, Rukmini would criticize her differently—"What does she care whether the children live or die? Without a mother, who will tell them not to eat too many sweets? If anything happens, I'll be the one to take responsibility. What does she care?"

If things had ended there, Nirmala might have tolerated it, but Rukmini began behaving like a secret policeman, monitoring her every move. If Nirmala stood on the terrace, Rukmini assumed she was looking at someone. If she spoke to a maid, Rukmini was sure she was gossiping. If she bought anything from the market, it had to be something indulgent. Rukmini would try to read her letters, listen in on her conversations. Nirmala lived in constant fear of her dual-edged sword.

One day, she could bear it no longer and spoke to Totaram: "Please speak to Didi. Why does she keep tormenting me?"

Totaram, his temper flaring, asked, "Has she said something to you?"

Nirmala: "She says something every day. It's impossible to say a word. If she's upset because I am managing the household funds, then give her the money instead. I don't want it. Let her remain the mistress of the house. I just don't want anyone taunting me." Tears welled up in Nirmala's eyes as she spoke.

Totaram saw this as an opportunity to show his love. He said, "I will deal with her today. I'll tell her clearly—either she stays here quietly, or she leaves. You are the mistress of this house, not her. She is only here to help you. If she troubles you instead, she doesn't need to stay here. I thought she was a widow, alone in the world—what harm could she do, eating a bit of our food? When other servants are fed here, why not my own sister? Besides, we needed someone to look after the children, so I let her stay. But that doesn't mean she can rule over you."

Nirmala added, "She tells the children to come to me for money. They pester me constantly, one thing after another. I can't rest for a moment. If I scold them, she rushes in, her eyes blazing. She thinks I'm jealous of them. God knows how much I love those children. They are practically my own. Why would I be jealous of them?"

Totaram was furious. "If any of those boys trouble you, beat them. I can see they're becoming unruly. I'll send Mansaram to the boarding house today, and I'll deal with the other two right now."

Totaram was on his way to court at that moment, so he had no time for scolding. But when he returned, he immediately confronted Rukmini. "Sister, do you want to stay here or not? If you want to stay, stay quietly. Don't make life difficult for others."

Rukmini understood that Nirmala had struck first. But she was not one to be easily intimidated. She was older, and she had spent her life serving this household. Who could dare evict her? She was astonished at her brother's pettiness. "Do you want me to be a slave here? If you want a slave, I won't be one in this house. If you want me to stand by quietly while someone sets fire to this house, or if I see someone straying and say nothing, then that won't be me. Why are you so upset? Have you lost all your wisdom? A young girl pulls the strings, and you draw your sword like a puppet?"

Totaram said, "I hear you're always taunting her, picking on her for every little thing. If you want to correct someone, do it kindly, in sweet words. Taunts only make things worse."

Rukmini replied, "So, you don't want me to say anything? Fine, but don't complain later that I didn't advise you. If my words are poison, why should I speak at all? Let's see how your new wife runs this household!"

At that moment, Siyaram and Jiyaram returned from school. They went straight to their aunt, asking for food.

Rukmini said, "Why don't you go ask your new mother? I'm not allowed to speak."

Totaram shouted, "If either of you sets foot in that room, I'll break your legs. You think you can get away with anything?"

Jiyaram, who was a bit bold, said, "You never say anything to her, and you scold us instead. She never gives us any money."

Siyaram added, "She says if we bother her, she'll cut our ears off. Isn't that right, Jiya?"

From her room, Nirmala called out, "When did I ever say I'd cut your ears off? Already lying at such a young age?"

Hearing this, Totaram grabbed Siyaram by both ears and lifted him up. The boy screamed in pain. Rukmini rushed over, pulling the child away from Totaram's grasp. "Stop it! Do you want to kill the boy? Look at his ears—they're red! It's true—once a man gets a new wife, he goes blind. If this is how things are now, God save this household!"

Nirmala was secretly pleased by her small victory, but when Totaram grabbed the child's ears, she couldn't hold back. She rushed to free the boy, but Rukmini got there first.

"First you started the fire, now you want to put it out? Just wait until you have children of your own—then you'll understand. How could you know another's pain?"

Nirmala said, "Here I am—ask them yourself. What did I say to them? All I said was that they keep bothering me for money. If I said anything else, may I lose my sight."

Totaram added, "I see how naughty these boys have become—I'm not blind. All three of them are stubborn and unruly. I'll send Mansaram to the hostel today."

Rukmini scoffed, "Until now, you never noticed any naughtiness. Now your eyes are suddenly wide open?"

Totaram retorted, "You're the one who's spoiled them."

Rukmini shot back, "So, I'm the root of all evil. Because of me, your household is ruined. Fine, I'm leaving. They're your children—beat them, kill them, I won't say a word."

Seeing the child crying, Nirmala was overwhelmed. She took him in her arms, cuddling him, and brought him to her room, trying to comfort him. But the boy continued to sob. His innocent heart could not feel the motherly love he had lost. This affection wasn't true love—it was mere pity. It was something given as charity, not as his right. His father had hit him once or twice before, when his mother was alive, but back then, she would stop speaking to him, showing her displeasure until he, having forgotten his offense, would return to her. He understood being punished for his mischief, but he did not understand being cuddled after being beaten. True motherly love had a certain harshness, softened with affection. This pity was different—it lacked the firmness of real love.

When the body is healthy, no one cares for it, but when it's hurt, efforts are made to protect it from further pain. Nirmala's compassion only reminded Siyaram of his mother's absence. He sat crying in her lap for a long time until he eventually fell asleep. When Nirmala tried to lay him on the cot, he clung to her neck, even in his sleep, as if afraid of falling into an abyss. His face twisted in fear. Nirmala held him tightly, unable to put him down.

In that moment, as she cradled the child, she felt a strange satisfaction she had never experienced before. For the first time, she felt the awakening of a deep awareness. Her path became clear, and she began to understand her true duty.

# Chapter - 6

*If you are expecting happy moments and fulfilling relationships, perhaps you would be better off reading a different story. This story is a portrayal of hope that keeps fading away, masked bravado, and unfulfilled desires. Munshi Totaram's relentless attempts to win over Nirmala's heart, and her quiet resilience, take us deeper into the murky waters of a complicated relationship where love and sympathy intermingle with pity and frustration. Brace yourself for yet another story where expectations are crushed, and love struggles to find a place amidst the chaos.*

After that day, when Munshi Totaram had tried to prove his love so convincingly, he had hoped that he would win Nirmala's heart. But his hopes were hardly fulfilled. Where once Nirmala used to occasionally smile and talk to him, she now became entirely occupied with the care of the children. Whenever he returned home, he would find the children around her. Sometimes he would see her bringing them in, sometimes dressing them, playing games with them, or telling them stories.

Nirmala's longing heart, having lost hope in romantic affection, found solace in her bond with the children. Talking and laughing with them fulfilled her maternal imagination. The hesitation, dislike, and reluctance she felt in conversing with her husband—sometimes even wanting to get up and leave—was replaced with the pure and simple affection she received from the children. Her heart was content.

Earlier, Mansaram was hesitant to approach her. Though he was almost the same age as his new mother, his mental development was five years behind. Hockey and football were his entire world—the playground for his imagination and a blooming garden for his desires. He was a slender, cheerful, and shy boy who only came home for meals and spent the rest of the day wandering. Listening to his stories of games, Nirmala would momentarily forget her worries and wished that those days could come back, when she used to play with dolls and marry them off—those days that seemed so recent and yet felt so distant.

Munshi Totaram, like many solitary men, had his desires. For some time, he had taken Nirmala out for walks and entertainment, but when he saw no fruitful result, he withdrew back into solitude. After the long, tiring hours of his daily work, he yearned for some joy and relaxation, but upon returning to what he considered his garden of happiness—now filled with wilted flowers, dried plants, and dust-covered petals —he often felt like giving up on it altogether. He could not understand why Nirmala remained indifferent toward him. He had tried every possible means a husband could use to win his wife's affection, but nothing seemed to work. He was clueless about what to do next.

One day, lost in his thoughts, his old friend Nayansukh Ram came to visit. After the usual greetings, Nayansukh smiled and said, "So, things must be great these days? Enjoying the embrace of your young wife must feel like reliving your youth, right? You're so fortunate! Nothing reconciles a fading youth better than a new marriage. But here I am, stuck—my wife clings to me so tightly that I can't even get a break. I'm considering a second marriage myself. If you come across a good match, let me know. I'll treat you to some paan made by her own hands!"

Totaram, with a serious expression, replied, "Don't make such a foolish mistake; you'll regret it. Young women are only happy with young men. We are no longer fit for this. Honestly, I'm regretting my second marriage—it's just become a burden. I thought I could enjoy a few more years, but it's turned out to be too much to handle."

Nayansukh chuckled, "What are you saying? It's not hard to win over young women—just take them for some outings, praise their beauty, and they're charmed."

Totaram sighed, "I've tried everything."

Nayansukh persisted, “Really? Perfumes, flowers, treats, outings—did you try all that?”

Totaram replied, “Yes, all of it. I’ve tried every trick in the book, but it’s all just nonsense.”

Nayansukh offered, “Alright, listen to me. Why don’t you improve your appearance a bit? There’s an ‘electric doctor’ in town these days who can remove all signs of aging—no wrinkles, no gray hair. They do something magical, transforming you entirely.”

Totaram asked, “How much does it cost?”

Nayansukh replied, “I heard it’s around five hundred rupees.”

Totaram scoffed, “He must be a fraud, fooling people with some temporary cream. If it were ten or twenty rupees, I might have tried it for fun. But five hundred rupees is too much.”

Nayansukh laughed, “For you, five hundred rupees is nothing. It’s just one month’s income. If I had five hundred rupees, it’d be my first investment—one hour of youth is worth much more than that.”

Totaram responded, “Why don’t you suggest something cheaper—some herbal remedy that could work without any cost? Leave these extravagant things to the rich.”

Nayansukh suggested with a grin, “Then play the role of a gallant man. Ditch that loose shirt; wear a stylish, tailored coat, pleated trousers, a gold chain around your neck, a Jaipuri turban on your head, surma in your eyes, and henna oil in your hair. You need to flatten that belly a bit—wear a double waistband if needed. It might be uncomfortable, but it’ll make your outfit look amazing. I’ll get you some hair dye. Memorize a few ghazals and recite them at the right moments. Your words should be dripping with charm, as if nothing matters in the world but your beloved. Look for opportunities to show bravery. At night, make some noise—yell ‘thief, thief!’ and go after them alone with a sword. Just make sure there’s no real thief, or you could end up looking foolish. If there is a thief, stay quiet and act like you didn’t even notice. Then, as soon as he runs away, jump out and chase, shouting ‘Where? Where?’ Try my advice for a month, and if she doesn’t start admiring you, I’ll pay you whatever fine you set.”

Totaram laughed it off at the time, as any sensible man would, but some of the words took root in his mind. Slowly, he began to change his appearance, trying not to draw attention. He started with dyeing his hair, then using surma in his eyes, and within a couple of months, his entire look had transformed. The idea of memorizing ghazals was absurd, but boasting about his bravery caused no harm. From that day, he began to weave tales of his bravery every day.

Nirmala started to worry—perhaps he was losing his sanity. A man who could barely digest moong dal with a couple of chapatis, trying to act gallant, was enough to raise suspicion. His new antics did not impress Nirmala at all; instead, she started to feel pity for him. Her feelings of anger and contempt faded away—those are reserved for those in their senses. A madman deserves only sympathy. She started teasing him, making jokes as people often do with someone who’s lost their mind. But she was careful not to let him realize it. She thought, poor man, he’s trying to atone for his mistakes. All this pretense is only to make me forget my sorrows. Now that fate cannot be changed, why should I make him suffer?

One evening, around nine, Totaram came home dressed like a young dandy and said to Nirmala, “Today, I had an encounter with three thieves. I had gone towards Shivpur, and it was dark. As I reached the railway road, three men, swords in hand, appeared out of nowhere. Believe me, they were like three black demons. I was alone, with just this stick. Facing those three with swords made my heart race—I knew my time was up. But I thought, if I have to die, let it be a hero’s death. One of them shouted, ‘Give us everything you have, and walk away quietly.’ I readied my stick and replied, ‘I only have this stick, and its worth is a man’s head.’ As soon as I said that, they lunged at me, and I blocked their strikes with my stick. For ten minutes, we fought intensely. Eventually, they realized they wouldn't succeed, so they sheathed their swords and said, 'Young man, we haven't seen someone as brave as you before. We've looted entire villages, but today you humbled us.' And then they disappeared."

Nirmala, with a serious smile, asked, "So there must be plenty of sword marks on this stick?"

Totaram, unprepared for this question, quickly replied, "I blocked all their strikes. A few hit the stick, but they glanced off, leaving no mark."

Before he could finish his sentence, Rukmini Devi came rushing in, panting, "Totaram, are you there? There's a snake in my room, right under my bed! I got up and ran. It must be two yards long, with its hood spread, hissing away. Please come quickly—bring a stick."

Totaram's face turned pale, his expression changed, but trying to mask his fear, he said, "A snake here? You must be mistaken—it's probably just a rope."

Rukmini insisted, "No, I saw it with my own eyes. Just come and see, will you? Are you afraid, being a man?"

Munshiji stepped out of the room, but then hesitated in the veranda. His feet felt heavy, and his heart pounded. Snakes are dangerous creatures—one bite, and you could lose your life for nothing. He muttered, "I'm not afraid. It's just a snake, not a lion. But sticks don't work on snakes—let me send someone to bring a spear." Saying this, Munshiji rushed out.

Mansaram was eating his dinner. Munshiji left, but Mansaram put down his meal, grabbed his hockey stick, and boldly entered the room. He immediately pulled the bed aside. The snake was alert, raising its hood instead of fleeing. Mansaram quickly threw the bedsheet over the snake and struck it repeatedly with the stick until the snake writhed beneath the cloth. He then lifted it on the stick and carried it outside. Munshiji, who was returning with a few others, saw

Mansaram holding the snake and let out a shriek before composing himself. He said, “I was coming—why did you hurry? Hand it over; someone can throw it away.” Then, with a show of bravery, Munshiji stood at Rukmini’s door, inspecting the room thoroughly, and with a twist of his mustache, he went to Nirmala and said, “By the time I got here, Mansaram had already killed it. Foolish boy ran in with just a stick. Snakes should always be killed with a spear—that’s the problem with boys. I’ve killed countless snakes—fed them until they were full, then crushed them with my bare hands.”

Rukmini scoffed, “Oh, we’ve seen your bravery.”

Munshiji, embarrassed, said, “Fine, call me a coward if you want. I’m not asking for any reward.” He then called out to the cook, “Serve the food.” Munshiji went to eat, while Nirmala stood at the doorway, deep in thought—“Oh God, is he really losing his mind? Does he want to make my situation even more miserable? I can serve him, respect him, offer my life at his feet, but I cannot do what is beyond me. I cannot erase the difference in our ages. What is it that he wants from me—I understand now. Ah, if only I had realized it sooner, he wouldn’t have had to go through all this pretense, all this struggle.”

## Chapter - 7

*If you're looking for a story where love conquers all, misunderstandings melt away effortlessly, and everyone finds their happily ever after, this story might not be for you. Instead, you'll find a household wrapped in suspicion, where even the most genuine intentions are tangled in the thorns of doubt. This is a tale of fragile relationships, struggling under the weight of hidden feelings and half-truths, where warmth and coldness live together, and every step forward seems to lead deeper into a maze of mistrust.*

From that day onward, Nirmala's demeanor began to change. She resolved to devote herself entirely to her duties. Until now, caught in the bitterness of despair, she had paid no attention to her responsibilities. Her heart had been consumed by a fiery turmoil, whose unbearable pain had left her almost senseless. But now, that storm began to calm. She realized that there was no joy left in her life. Why should she destroy this life in pursuit of an illusion? Not all beings in this world are destined for a bed of roses. She was one of those unfortunate souls burdened with sorrow. This burden could not be lifted; even if she wished to throw it away, it wasn't possible. Regardless of whether her vision darkened, her neck broke, or her legs gave out from carrying this heavy load, she had to bear it. How long could a prisoner of fate cry? Even if she cried, who would witness her tears? Who would show her pity? Instead, weeping would only make her work harder and bring more suffering.

The next day, when Munshi Totaram returned from the court, he saw Nirmala, her face bright with a smile, standing at the door of her room. Her radiant presence filled his eyes with satisfaction. After many days, he saw this blossomed lotus again. In the room, a large mirror hung on the wall, usually covered by a curtain. Today, the curtain had been lifted. When Totaram stepped into the room, his eyes fell upon his own reflection in the mirror. He was struck. The fatigue of the day's work had dulled his face, and despite eating various nutritious foods, wrinkles were visible on his cheeks. His belly protruded like an unruly horse, despite his efforts to keep it in check. Standing in front of the mirror, but facing away, was Nirmala. The difference between the two of them was glaring—one, a majestic palace adorned with gems; the other, a crumbling ruin. He couldn't bear to look at himself in the mirror. His own wretched state was unbearable to him. He stepped away from the mirror, feeling disgusted by his own appearance. No wonder this beautiful woman despised him. He couldn't even bring himself to look at Nirmala; her flawless beauty had become a thorn in his heart.

Nirmala spoke, "Why are you so late today? I've been waiting all day, my eyes straining."

Totaram, looking towards the window, replied, "The cases kept me so busy I didn't get a moment's rest. There was still one more case, but I pretended to have a headache and ran away."

Nirmala smiled, "Why do you take on so many cases? You should only work as much as you can comfortably manage. It's not worth working yourself to death. Please, don't take so many cases. I have no greed for money. If you live in comfort, we'll have enough."

Totaram shrugged, "But how can I turn away money when it comes to me?"

Nirmala responded, "If wealth comes at the cost of flesh and blood, it's better it doesn't come at all. I don't hunger for riches."

At that moment, Mansaram also returned from school. Drops of sweat glistened on his face from walking in the sun, and a rosy blush ran across his fair cheeks. His eyes seemed to radiate a glow. Standing at the door, he called, "Mother, please give me something to eat. I need to go play."

Nirmala brought a glass of water and a plate with some dry fruits for Mansaram. After eating, as he was about to leave, she asked, "When will you be back?"

Mansaram replied, "I can't say for sure. We have a hockey match against the whites. The barracks are far from here."

Nirmala said, "Come back soon, dear. If the food gets cold, you'll say you're not hungry."

Mansaram looked at Nirmala with innocent affection and said, "If I'm late, just assume I ate there. There's no need to wait for me."

After he left, Nirmala said, "He used to never come home. He used to feel shy talking to me. If he needed something, he'd send for it from outside. Ever since I called him and talked to him, he's been coming around."

Totaram said with irritation, "Why does he come to you for food? Why doesn't he ask my elder sister?"

Nirmala had mentioned this out of a desire for praise, wanting to show how much she cared for Totaram's children. This wasn't feigned love—she genuinely had affection for the children. Her character still retained a childlike quality—curiosity, restlessness, and a love for playful activities. These traits blossomed around the children. The jealousy often found in wives had not yet awakened in her heart. But instead of being pleased, her husband frowned. Not understanding the intent behind his displeasure, she said, "How would I know why he doesn't ask them? He comes to me, and I don't refuse him. If I did, then people would say I hate the children."

Totaram didn't respond to this, but that day, he didn't chat with his clients either. Instead, he went straight to Mansaram and began testing him on his studies. This was the first time in his life that Totaram had taken such an interest in Mansaram's or any child's education. He never had the time, being too absorbed in his work. It had been almost forty years since he'd studied those subjects himself. Since then, he hadn't even glanced at them. He only read legal books and documents, and never had the time for anything else. But today, he began questioning Mansaram on those subjects. Mansaram was both intelligent and diligent. Despite being the captain of his sports team, he ranked first in his class. Whatever lesson he saw once was etched in his memory like a line carved in stone.

In his impatience, Totaram couldn't think of insightful questions—questions that would make even a clever boy think—and Mansaram answered the simple ones without any trouble. Just like a soldier getting more furious after a missed strike, Totaram grew increasingly irritated at Mansaram's quick responses. He wanted to ask a question that would stump Mansaram, to find his weakness. He was no longer satisfied with knowing what Mansaram could do—he wanted to see what he couldn't do. An experienced examiner might have easily found Mansaram's weaknesses, but Totaram, relying on his half-century-old forgotten knowledge, wasn't successful.

In the end, when he found no excuse to vent his frustration, he said, "I see you roaming around aimlessly all day. I judge your character to be worse than your intelligence, and I cannot tolerate this kind of aimless wandering."

Mansaram replied fearlessly, "Except for an hour in the evening when I go to play, I don't go anywhere. You can ask mother or aunt. I don't like wandering around myself. But the headmaster insists I come to play, so I have to. If you don't want me to play, I won't go from tomorrow."

Seeing that the conversation was turning against him, Totaram spoke sharply, "How can I be sure that you don't roam around except to play? I keep hearing complaints."

Mansaram, getting riled up, asked, "Who made such a complaint? Let me know, and I'll confront them."

Totaram replied, "It doesn't matter who it is. You should have enough faith that I wouldn't accuse you falsely."

Mansaram said, "If someone comes forward and says they saw me wandering, I won't show my face again."

Totaram sneered, "Why would anyone want to come forward, knowing that you'd retaliate by breaking the tiles on their roof with your friends? I haven't heard this from just one person—many have said it. I have no reason to distrust my friends. I want you to stay in the boarding house."

Mansaram hung his head and said, "I have no objection to staying there. Just tell me when to leave."

Totaram taunted, "Why the long face? Don't you like staying there? It looks as though the thought of it terrifies you. What's the matter? What trouble would you face there?"

Mansaram wasn't keen on staying in the hostel, but since Totaram had brought it up and asked him about it, he masked his hesitation with cheerfulness and said, "Why would I sulk? It's the same for me as a boarding house. There's no problem, and if there is, I can manage. I'll leave tomorrow—if there's space available."

Totaram, being a lawyer, understood the hidden meaning—that the boy was looking for an excuse not to go while saving face. He said, "There's room for everyone except you?"

Mansaram replied, "There are quite a few boys who didn't get rooms and are renting houses outside. Just recently, when a spot opened up in the hostel, fifty applications came in for it."

Totaram didn't think it wise to argue further. He ordered Mansaram to be ready the next day and had his carriage prepared to go out for a ride. Lately, he'd taken up the habit of going for a ride in the evenings—a wise soul had advised him that nothing promotes longevity better.

After Totaram left, Mansaram went to Rukmini and said, "Aunt, father wants me to start staying at school from tomorrow."

Rukmini asked in surprise, "Why?"

Mansaram shrugged, "How would I know? He said I wander around here like a vagabond."

Rukmini was indignant, "Didn't you tell him that you don't go anywhere?"

Mansaram replied, "Of course I did, but he wouldn't believe me."

Rukmini shook her head, "This must be your new mother's doing."

Mansaram defended her, "No, Aunt. I don't think it's her. She never says anything bad about me. If I need something, she immediately gives it."

Rukmini muttered, "You don't understand women's wiles. She must be behind all this. Just wait, I'll go and ask her."

Rukmini stormed to Nirmala's room. She wouldn't let go of an opportunity to take Nirmala to task, hurling accusations, taunting her, and making her cry. Nirmala respected her, feared her, and never answered back. She had hoped that Rukmini would offer guidance, correct her when she went wrong, and oversee all the household tasks. But Rukmini remained antagonistic towards her.

Nirmala stood up from her bed and said, "Please, sit down, Sister."

Rukmini, standing, shot back, "Are you planning to drive everyone out of the house and live here alone?"

Nirmala, her face filled with distress, asked, "What happened, Sister? I haven't said anything to anyone."

Rukmini retorted, "You're driving Mansaram out of the house, and then you say you haven't done anything? Can't you tolerate even that much?"

Nirmala pleaded, "Sister, I swear on your feet, I don't know anything. May I go blind if I've said anything against him."

Rukmini sneered, "Why swear falsely? Totaram never used to scold the boy before. Once, when Mansaram had gone to his grandmother's for a week, he was so anxious that he went to bring him back himself. And now, he wants to throw that same Mansaram into a hostel. If even a hair on that boy's head is harmed, you'll see. He has never stayed outside. He forgets to eat, forgets to dress, falls asleep wherever he sits. He may look grown, but his nature is still that of a child. He'll be miserable in the hostel. Who's going to care whether he's eaten or lost something, where he's put his clothes, or where he sleeps? If no one cares for him at home, who's going to care outside? I've warned you—now you do as you please."

Saying this, Rukmini stormed off.

When Totaram returned from his ride, Nirmala brought up the subject immediately, "I've been studying a bit of English with Mansaram lately. If he leaves, it will disrupt my studies. Who else will teach me?"

Until now, Totaram hadn't known about this. Nirmala had thought that once she had practiced enough, she'd surprise him by speaking English fluently. She had learned a little from her brothers before, but now she was studying regularly. Totaram felt a chill run through him; his expression darkened as he asked, "Since when has he been teaching you? You never told me."

Nirmala had only seen this expression on his face once before, when he had nearly beaten Siyaram senseless. Today, it returned, more terrifying than before. Timidly, she replied, "It doesn't interfere with his studies. I only ask him to teach me when he's free. I always ask if it would disrupt his work, and if he says yes, I let it be. Often, I just hold him back for ten minutes before he goes to play. I make sure not to affect his performance."

It was a small matter, but Totaram, dejected, fell back onto the bed, his head in his hands. The situation was worse than he had imagined. He cursed himself for not making arrangements to send Mansaram away sooner. Now he understood the reason behind the newfound cheerfulness in his wife. The room had never been so neat and decorated before. She had never dressed herself up like this before, but now it seemed as if she had undergone a transformation. He even considered throwing Mansaram out immediately, but his mature mind told him that this wasn't the right moment for anger. If she sensed anything, it would be disastrous. He needed to probe her feelings first.

He said, "I understand that teaching you for a few minutes doesn't disrupt his work, but he's a wayward boy. It gives him an excuse not to study. If he fails his exams, he'll say he spent all day teaching you. I'll hire a governess for you. It won't be much extra expense. You should have asked me earlier. What could he possibly teach you? He probably just tells you a few words and then runs off. That way, you won't learn anything."

Nirmala immediately countered, "No, that's not true. He teaches me with dedication, and his style is such that I actually enjoy learning. You should see how he explains things one day. I doubt a governess would teach with as much attention."

Totaram, twirling his mustache in satisfaction at his questioning skills, asked, "Does he teach you once a day or multiple times?"

Nirmala still did not understand the intention behind these questions and replied, "Initially, he only taught me in the evenings, but for the past few days, he's also been coming by once to check my writing. He says he's the best in his class. He just came first in the recent exams, so how can you say he isn't focused on his studies? Besides, I'm saying this so that Sister doesn't think I've stirred up trouble. I don't want her taunting me for no reason. She just stormed out after scolding me."

Totaram thought, "I understand very well. You're just a girl, and you're trying to manipulate me. You want to use Sister as an excuse to get your way." He said aloud, "I don't understand why the thought of the boarding house terrifies him. Most boys are thrilled to be with their friends, but he cries instead. Not long ago, he was fully committed to his studies. His recent success is the result of that hard work. But lately, he's been bitten by the bug of leisure. If I don't curb it now, it'll be impossible to manage later. I'll hire a governess for you."

The next morning, Totaram got dressed and went out. Several clients were waiting in the drawing room, including a minister, who paid Totaram several thousand rupees in fees each year. But Totaram left them sitting there, promising to return in ten minutes, and took his carriage straight to the headmaster's house. The headmaster was a kind man who received him warmly, but unfortunately, there was no space for another student in the hostel. All the rooms were full. The education inspector had given strict orders to prioritize students from out of town over those from the city. Therefore, even if a space opened up, Mansaram wouldn't be eligible, as many out-of-town students were already on the waiting list.

Totaram was a lawyer, accustomed to dealing with people who, driven by greed, could turn the impossible into the possible. He thought perhaps some money might solve the issue, so he tried having a discreet conversation with the office clerk. But the clerk laughed and said, "Munshiji, this isn’t a courtroom; it’s a school. If the headmaster gets wind of this, he’ll be furious and expel Mansaram immediately. He might even complain to the authorities."

Helpless Totaram left, feeling defeated. By ten o'clock, he returned home, annoyed. Mansaram was just leaving for school. Totaram gave him a stern look, as though Mansaram were his enemy, and walked inside.

For the next ten to twelve days, Totaram’s routine remained the same. He would meet with one headmaster or another, either in the morning or evening, trying to get Mansaram into a boarding house, but there was no space available. Everywhere he went, he received the same response. There were only two options left: either rent a separate house for Mansaram or admit him to another school. Both options were feasible. Schools in smaller towns often had vacancies. But now Totaram’s suspicions had somewhat eased.

From that day onward, he never saw Mansaram inside the house again. Mansaram even stopped going out to play. Before school, and after returning, he would stay in his room. It was summer, and even standing in the open fields would make one sweat profusely, yet Mansaram didn’t step out of his room. His sense of dignity burned to rid himself of the accusation of aimlessness. He was determined to prove his innocence through his behavior.

One day, Totaram was having his meal, and Mansaram came in after bathing, ready to eat. Totaram hadn’t seen him bare-chested in months. Today, when he looked at Mansaram, he was stunned. A skeleton stood before him. Although his face still shone with the glow of self-control, his body had withered away. Totaram asked, "Are you unwell these days? Why are you so thin?"

Mansaram, wrapping a cloth around himself, replied, "No, I'm perfectly fine."

Totaram persisted, "Then why are you so thin?"

Mansaram answered, "I'm not thin. I've never been fatter than this."

Totaram retorted, "Nonsense, you're half the size you were, and you say you're not thin? What do you think, Sister?"

Rukmini, standing in the courtyard, pouring water on the basil plant, said, "Why would he be thin? He's being well looked after now. I was a simpleton who didn't know how to care for children. I spoiled their habits by giving them snacks. Now, a well-educated, clever woman is caring for them like they're precious jewels. If anyone is thinner, it's her enemy."

Totaram protested, "Sister, you're being unfair. Who told you that you were spoiling the children? The work others can't do should be done by you. You can't just abandon your duties. How can a young girl take care of the children? That's your responsibility."

Rukmini replied, "I cared for them as long as I felt they were mine. When you decided I wasn't part of the family, why should I cling to you? Ask him, how many days has it been since he drank milk? Go check his room—the sweets you sent for his breakfast are rotting there. The mistress thinks her duty is done once she sets the food out. Brother, children who have never known affection might grow up like this, but your boys have always been pampered like precious jewels. They can't suddenly be treated like orphans and still be content. I'm speaking plainly. Let anyone be offended; what can i do? I hear you're planning to send the boy to a hostel. The poor boy is even afraid to come to me now, and even if he did, what would I have left to give him?"

Just then, Mansaram finished eating his two flatbreads and stood up. Totaram asked, "What, only two flatbreads? You haven't even been sitting for a minute. What did you eat? You only took two flatbreads."

Mansaram hesitantly replied, "There was also some lentils and vegetables. If I eat more, my throat starts burning, and I get sour belches."

Munshiji got up from his meal, very worried. If this keeps up, he might fall seriously ill. He was very angry at Rukmini at this moment. Her grievance was that she was not the mistress of the house. Doesn't she understand what right she has to be the mistress of the house? How can a person who doesn't even know how to manage money be the mistress? She was the mistress for a year, but she couldn't save a single penny. Rupkala (his first wife) would save two to two-and-a-half hundred rupees out of the same income. Under her rule, that same income couldn't even cover the expenses. It doesn't matter; her pampering has spoiled these children. These grown-up boys do not need to be fed when they can feed themselves. They should take care of themselves.

Munshiji spent the entire day pondering over this issue. He even discussed it with two or four friends. People advised him not to restrict his play and games, not to confine him from now on. In the open air, the chance of corrupt character is less than in a closed room. Definitely protect him from bad company, but that doesn't mean not allowing him to leave the house. Loneliness during youth is extremely harmful to one's character.

Now Munshiji realized his mistake. He returned home and went to Mansaram. He had just come back from school and, without changing clothes, had opened a book and was staring out of the window. His gaze was fixed on a beggar woman holding her child, begging for alms. The child was sitting in his mother's lap, looking so happy, as if he was sitting on a royal throne. Seeing the child, Mansaram started crying. Isn't this child happier than me? What thing in this endless universe could he get that would make him happier than being in this lap? Even God could not create such a thing. Why does God even create such children who are destined to suffer the pain of being separated from their mothers? Who is more unfortunate in this world than me today? Who cares about whether I eat, drink, live, or die? If I were to die today, whose heart would be hurt? Father now finds pleasure in making me cry; he doesn't even want to see my face and is making preparations to throw me out of the house. Oh, mother. Your dear son has become a vagabond today. The same father, into whose hands you entrusted us three brothers, today calls me a vagabond and a scoundrel. I am not even worthy of living in this house. Thinking this, Mansaram broke into uncontrollable sobs.

At that very moment, Totaram entered the room and stood there. Mansaram hurriedly wiped away his tears and stood with his head lowered. Munshiji might have stepped into his room for the first time. Mansaram's heart started pounding, wondering what trouble awaited him today. Munshiji saw him crying, and for a moment, his paternal affection startled him awake from sleep. He said anxiously, "Why, why are you crying, son? Did someone say something to you?"

Mansaram somehow managed to control his tears and replied, "No, I am not crying."

Munshiji: "Did your mother say something to you?"

Mansaram: "No, she doesn't even talk to me."

Munshiji: "What can I do, son? I got married hoping that you would get a mother, but that hope hasn't been fulfilled. So, she doesn't talk to you at all?"

Mansaram: "No, she hasn't talked to me for months."

Munshiji: "Strange woman. It's hard to understand what she wants. If I had known her nature, I wouldn't have married her. She picks a new quarrel every day. She told me that you're always disappearing somewhere all day. How could I know her real feelings? I thought you might be wandering around all day in bad company. Which father would not be hurt to see his beloved son roaming around like a vagabond? That's why I decided to put you in a boarding house. Nothing else, son. I don't want to stop your playing and having fun. Seeing you like this breaks my heart. Yesterday, I realized I was mistaken. Play as much as you like. Go out in the morning and evening. Fresh air will do you good. Whatever you need, ask me, not her. Think of her as if she's not even there. Your mother may have left, but I am still here."

The innocent, simple-hearted child was overwhelmed by his father's love. It felt as if God himself was standing there. Torn by despair and anguish, he had thought his father to be heartless and whatnot. He had no complaints against his stepmother. Now he realized how unjust he had been towards his godlike father. A wave of filial devotion surged in his heart, and he fell at his father's feet, crying.

Munshiji was moved with compassion. The son whom he couldn't bear to be away from for even a moment, whose virtue, intellect, and character everyone praised, why had his heart turned so cold towards him? He had started seeing his beloved son as an enemy and was ready to exile him. Nirmala was the wall standing between father and son. To draw Nirmala closer to him, he had to withdraw from the other side, which only widened the gap between father and son. As a result, today the situation had become such that he had to deceive his beloved son to this extent. After much thought, an idea occurred to him, one that he hoped would allow him to remove Nirmala from the middle and draw his estranged child closer. He had even begun implementing that plan, though whether it would succeed or not, only time would tell.

From the day Totaram, after much pleading from Nirmala, decided to send Mansaram to the boarding house, she had stopped being teached by him and had not even spoken to him. She had sensed her husband's distrustful attitude to some extent. "Oh! Such a suspicious mind. May God protect the dignity of this house." She thought to herself, "Do they think so despicable of me?" Pondering over such thoughts, she wept for several days.

Then she started thinking, what are they suspicious of? What is it about me that bothers them so much? Even after much thought, she couldn't find anything in herself that seemed offensive. Is it her teaching Mansaram, her laughing and talking with him that causes their suspicion? Should she stop studying by him, stop even talking to him, and never look at his face again? But such a penance seemed impossible for her. Talking and laughing with Mansaram excited and fulfilled her imagination. She felt immense joy while talking to him, which she couldn't put into words. She had no impure intentions in her mind. She could not even dream of having a corrupt love for Mansaram. It was just a natural longing that every human being has for companionship, which found an unknown fulfillment in this. Now this unfulfilled longing began to burn in her heart like a lamp. Time and again, she would feel restless with an unknown pain, wandering around in search of something lost, sitting wherever she found herself, unable to engage in any work. Yet, when Munshiji came home, she submerged all her desires in despair and talked to him with a smile.

Yesterday, after Munshiji had finished his meal and left for court, Rukmini came and taunted Nirmala a lot. "You knew you would have to take care of children here. Then why didn't you tell your family not to marry you here? You should have gone to a place where there were no children, only a man who would be happy to see your beauty and charm, and count himself lucky. Do you think this old man is going to be infatuated with your looks and gestures? He married you to look after these children, not for pleasure." She kept sprinkling salt on her wounds for a long time, but Nirmala didn’t utter a word. She wanted to present her defense but couldn't. If she said that she was doing as her husband wished, the family's dirty laundry would be aired. If she admitted her mistake and tried to rectify it, who knew what consequences that would bring? Nirmala was generally very outspoken; she had no hesitation or fear in telling the truth. But at this delicate moment, she had no choice but to remain silent. There was no other way. She could see that Mansaram was very disheartened and miserable, and she also saw that he was getting weaker day by day. But her words and actions were sealed. It was as if a thief was suffering because his own house had been robbed; such was Nirmala's situation now.

# Chapter - 8

*If you seek the light of joyous moments and hearts coming together, you may find this chapter heavy with sorrow instead. Here, the silence between words deepens, and the weight of unfulfilled emotions tugs at fragile connections. Love stands on the precipice of despair, and each attempt to bridge the divide seems to pull hearts further apart. This is a tale of longing and loss, where the sweetness of solace is as elusive as the fading warmth of a setting sun.*

When something happens against our expectations, that is when sorrow arises. Mansaram never expected that Nirmala would complain about him, and that's why he felt such intense anguish. Why would she complain about me? What does she want? Is it that I live off her husband's earnings, that money is spent on my education, on my clothes? She must want me out of this house so that her expenses are reduced. She always seems so cordial to me. I've never heard a harsh word from her. Is this all just a facade? It could be. A hunter scatters grains to trap a bird. Ah, I never imagined that beneath the grain lay a snare, that this maternal affection was merely a prelude to my banishment.

Why does my presence bother her so? The man who is her husband—isn't he my father too? Is the bond between a father and son any less sacred than that between a man and wife? If I do not begrudge her absolute authority in the household, if she can do whatever she pleases without my saying a word, then why can't she spare me even a tiny space under this roof? She lives in a grand house; why can't she let me sit under the shade of a tree? Perhaps she fears that I might grow up to claim my father's property, so she wants me gone now. How can I convince her that she needn't worry? How can I tell her that Mansaram would rather take poison than harm her? No matter how many difficulties I have to face, I will never be a thorn in her heart.

Father may have given me life, and even now his affection for me hasn't completely faded, but do I not know that the day he married her, he cast us out from his heart? Now, we remain here like orphans—this house is no longer ours. Perhaps due to past attachments, we are treated a bit better than other orphans would be, but orphans we are all the same. We truly became orphans the day Mother passed away. And whatever was left, this marriage completed. I never sought a close bond with her anyway. If, during those days, she had complained about me to Father, it might not have hurt as much. I would have been prepared for that blow. I had a lot of affection for her. Yet, she struck me at my lowest. Even wild animals only attack humans when they find them defenseless.

Now I understand why I was pampered. If I ever delayed coming to eat, I would be called upon multiple times, breakfast would include delicacies, and I would often be asked, 'Do you need any money?' That's why she got me that watch for a hundred rupees. But was there no other complaint she could find than calling me wayward? What proof does she have of my delinquency? She could have said that I don't focus on my studies or that I ask for money too frequently, but why this? Perhaps because it's the harshest blow she could deal me. The first arrow she shot pierced me deeply, leaving me nowhere to turn. Was this so I would fall from Father's favor? Sending me to the boarding house was merely an excuse; the real aim was to discard me like a fly from milk. After a few months, they would stop providing for me—whether I lived or died wouldn't matter. If I had known this was her doing, I would have found a place to stay no matter how difficult it was—even the servants' quarters, even the veranda would have sufficed.

But now, dawn has broken. Since affection is gone, staying here just to fill my stomach would be shameless. This is no longer my home. I was born here, I played here, but it's no longer mine. Father is no longer my father, even though I am still his son. All relationships in the world are built on love—without love, they mean nothing. Oh, Mother, where are you? Thinking this, Mansaram began to cry. As memories of his mother's love resurfaced, tears began to flow. He called out 'Mother' several times, as if she were standing right there, listening to him. For the first time, he truly felt the agony of being motherless. He was proud, he was brave, but having been raised in comfort, he now felt completely abandoned.

It was ten o'clock at night. Munshiji was out attending a dinner. Twice, the maid had come to call Mansaram for dinner, but each time he had angrily told her, 'I'm not hungry, I won't eat anything. Stop bothering me!' And so, when Nirmala tried to send her again, she refused. 'Madam, he won't come if I call him.'

Nirmala asked, 'Why wouldn't he come? Just go tell him the food is getting cold—ask him to eat a few bites at least.'

The maid replied, 'I have tried everything, he just won't come.'

Nirmala pressed, 'Did you tell him that I'm waiting for him?'

The maid replied honestly, 'No, madam, I didn't say that. why should i lie'

'Well, go and tell him I am waiting for him. Tell him that if he doesn't eat, I won't put the kitchen away and rest either. My dear maid, go once more. If he still doesn't come, carry him on your back,' Nirmala said with a laugh.

With a bit of grumbling, the maid went, but came back in just a moment, alarmed, 'madam, he's crying. Did someone say something to him?'

Nirmala, shocked, stood up and took a few steps forward, as if a mother had heard that her child had fallen into a well. She paused and asked the maid, 'He's crying? Did you ask him why?'

The maid admitted, 'No, madam, I didn't ask. But he is crying.'

Alone, in this silent night, he was crying. Perhaps he missed his mother. How do I comfort him now? How? she thought, feeling helpless. Here, even a sneeze can cost you your dignity. God, you are my witness—if I have ever wronged him, may I bear the consequences. What can I do? He must think that I complained about him to Father. How can I convince him that I haven't spoken a word against him? If I were to wish ill upon such a virtuous young man, I would be the most monstrous being in the world.

Nirmala saw that Mansaram's health was deteriorating day by day. He grew weaker and weaker, his once bright face losing its glow, his laughter fading. She knew the reason, but she could say nothing to her husband. Watching it all, her heart ached, but her tongue remained tied. Sometimes she grew frustrated, wondering why Mansaram was so upset over such a small thing. Did being called 'wayward' make him one? It's different for me—a mere suspicion could ruin me, but why should he care about such trivial things?

She had an overwhelming desire to go to him, comfort him, and bring him food. Poor thing, he'll be hungry all night. Oh, I am the root of all this trouble. Before I came, there was peace in this house. Father doted on his children, and they adored him. Since I arrived, everything has turned upside down. What will be the end of all this? Only God knows. God won't even grant me death. Poor boy, lying there hungry, and he hardly eats anything anyway—no more than a toddler would. She decided to go. Against her husband's wishes, she went. Her heart trembled at the thought of comforting the boy who, by relationship, was like her son.

First, she checked Rukmini's room; she was fast asleep after dinner. Then she went to the outer room. It was silent there; Munshiji had not yet returned. After taking in everything, she went to Mansaram's room. The door was open. Mansaram was sitting at the desk, his head bowed over a book, looking like a living image of sorrow and despair.

Nirmala tried to call out to him, but no sound came from her throat. Suddenly, Mansaram lifted his head and looked towards the door. Seeing Nirmala in the dim light, he couldn't recognize her immediately and asked in surprise, 'Who is it?'

Nirmala's voice trembled as she said, 'It's me. Why aren't you coming to eat? It's quite late.'

Mansaram turned his face away, saying, 'I'm not hungry.'

Nirmala said, 'I've already heard that from the maid three times.'

Mansaram replied, 'Then hear it a fourth time from me.'

Nirmala persisted, 'You didn't eat anything in the evening either. Aren't you hungry?'

With a sarcastic laugh, Mansaram said, 'Even if I were hungry, where would it come from?'

Saying this, Mansaram tried to close the door, but Nirmala moved the door aside and entered the room. She took Mansaram's hand in hers and, with tearful eyes and a voice full of gentle pleading, said, 'Please, come eat a little, for my sake. If you don't eat, I too will stay hungry tonight. Just a couple of bites, please. Do you want me to starve all night?'

Mansaram hesitated. She hasn't eaten yet, waiting for me? Is this kindness, affection, and humility real, or is she an embodiment of envy and misfortune? He thought of his mother. When he used to sulk, she would come to comfort him in the same way, and she wouldn't leave until he complied. He could not refuse this appeal. He said, 'I regret that I've caused you so much trouble. If I had known you were waiting for me, I would have eaten earlier.'

Nirmala said with a touch of disdain, 'How could you imagine that you would stay hungry while I ate and slept peacefully? Just because I'm your stepmother, does that make me selfish?'

Suddenly, they heard Munshiji's cough from the men's room, suggesting he was coming towards Mansaram's room. Nirmala's face turned pale. She quickly left the room, and finding no opportunity to go inside, she spoke in a harsh tone, 'I am not a servant to sit by the kitchen door for anyone all night. If you don't want to eat, just say so earlier.'

Munshiji saw Nirmala standing there. 'What is this calamity? What are you doing here?' he asked.

Nirmala replied in a sharp tone, 'What am I doing? I'm lamenting my fate. I am the root of all evil in this house. Someone is sulking here, someone else is pouting there—how many people am I supposed to appease, and for how long?'

Munshiji, somewhat puzzled, asked, 'What's going on?'

Nirmala answered, 'He refuses to eat, that's all. I sent the maid ten times, and finally, I had to come myself. It's easy for him to say he's not hungry, but I'm just a servant in this house—everyone's ready to blame me. No one's hungry, but who can stop them from saying that the witch doesn't feed anyone?'

Munshiji turned to Mansaram, 'Why aren't you eating? Do you know what time it is?'

Mansaram stood there, bewildered. A mystery was unfolding before him, one he could not comprehend. The eyes that had been filled with tears of kindness a moment ago were now blazing with anger. The lips that had spoken so sweetly a moment ago were now spewing venom. In that state of half-consciousness, he replied, 'I am not hungry.'

Munshiji scolded, 'Why aren't you hungry? If you weren't hungry, why didn't you say so earlier? Who will sit up all night waiting for you? You didn't use to be like this. When did you learn to sulk? Go and eat.'

Mansaram replied, 'No, I am not hungry at all.'

Munshiji clenched his teeth and said, 'Fine, eat when you're hungry.' Saying this, he went inside. Nirmala followed him.

Munshiji went to lie down, and Nirmala put away the food, washed her hands, chewed some betel leaf, and returned smiling.

Munshiji asked, 'Did you eat?'

Nirmala replied, 'What else could I do? Should I leave my meal for anyone?'

Munshiji said, 'I don't know what has happened to him. He is fading away day by day, staying locked in that room all day.'

Nirmala said nothing. She was drowning in an ocean of worry. What must have gone through Mansaram's mind when he saw my sudden change in demeanor? Did he wonder why my expression changed the moment Father arrived? Did he understand the reason behind it? The poor boy was about to eat, and then Father appeared out of nowhere. How can I explain this mystery to him? Is it even possible to explain? What kind of predicament have I fallen into?

The next morning, Nirmala busied herself with the household chores. At around nine, maid came and said, 'Mansaram is loading all his papers and belongings onto a cart.'

Nirmala asked, 'What! did you ask him?'

Maid replied, 'I asked, and he said he's going to stay at the school now.'

Mansaram had gone to the headmaster of his school early that morning to arrange his accommodation. At first, the headmaster said, 'There's no room here; there are several other boys who've requested to stay before you.' But when Mansaram said, 'If I don't get a place, I may have to stop my studies and might not be able to take the exam,' the headmaster had to relent. Mansaram was expected to pass with distinction, and the teachers had faith that he would bring honor to the school. The headmaster couldn't turn away such a promising student, so he cleared out his office room for him. That's why Mansaram, upon returning, started loading his belongings onto a cart.

Munshiji asked, 'What's the hurry? You could go in a few days. I wanted to arrange a good cook for you.'

Mansaram replied, 'The cook there makes very good food.'

Munshiji advised, 'Take care of your health. Don't lose your health in the pursuit of studies.'

Mansaram assured, 'No one is allowed to study there after nine o'clock, and everyone has to follow the rules and play.'

Munshiji asked, 'Why are you leaving your bedding behind? What will you sleep on?'

Mansaram replied, 'I'm taking a blanket; I won't need a mattress.'

Munshiji said, 'While the porter is loading your things, why don't you eat something? You didn't eat anything last night either.'

Mansaram responded, 'I'll eat there. I've already told the cook to prepare something for me. Eating here would only delay me.'

At home, Jiyaram and Siyaram were insisting on going with their brother. Nirmala was trying to placate them, 'Children, young boys aren't allowed there; you have to do everything yourself.'

Suddenly, Rukmini entered and said, 'You have a heart of stone. The boy didn't eat last night, and now he's leaving without food, and here you are, talking to the children? Don't you understand him? Know that he's not just going to school—he's leaving for exile and won't come back. He's not the kind of boy who forgets everything after a game. Words carve deep lines on his heart.'

Nirmala said in a choked voice, 'What can I do, sister-in-law? He doesn't listen to anyone. Please, just go and call him back. He'll come if you call.'

Rukmini: "What exactly happened that made him leave? He never felt out of place in this house before. He never liked being anywhere else other than his own home. You must have said something to him, or perhaps complained about him. Why are you sowing thorns for yourself? You won't find peace after destroying this home."

Nirmala, in tears, said, "If I ever said anything to him, let my tongue be cut off. Yes, I am blamed only because I am a stepmother. I am begging you, please go and bring him back."

Rukmini said sharply, "Why don't you bring him back yourself? Would you become smaller by doing so? If he were your own, would you just sit like this?"

Nirmala was like a bird without wings, seeing a snake coming towards her, wanting to fly away but unable to do so, trying to jump and falling down, helplessly fluttering its wings. Her heart was in turmoil, but she could not step outside. Just then, both the boys came and said, "Brother has left."

Nirmala stood frozen, as if she had lost all her senses. He left? He didn't even come inside the house, didn't meet me before leaving. Such hatred for me. I may not be anything for him, but at least he should come inside to meet his aunt. I was right here, wasn't I? How could he step inside? He would have seen me. That is why he left.

## Chapter - 9

With Mansaram's departure, the house felt empty. The two younger boys were still attending the same school. Every day, Nirmala would ask them about Mansaram. She hoped that he would come home during the holidays. But when the holidays passed and he did not come, Nirmala grew anxious. She had made moong laddoos especially for him. On Monday morning, she sent maid with the laddoos to the school. At nine, maid returned, carrying the laddoos, untouched.

Nirmala asked, "Is he feeling any better now?"

Maid replied, "Better? No, he looks worse."

Nirmala’s worry deepened. "Is he unwell?" she asked.

Maid hesitated before answering, "I didn’t ask him that, madam, why would I lie? But the cook there is my brother-in-law, and he said that your Mansaram barely eats. He just takes a couple of flatbreads and doesn’t touch anything else all day. He’s always studying."

Nirmala was deeply concerned. "Did you ask him why he returned the laddoos?"

Again, Maid replied, "No, madam, it didn’t occur to me to ask. But he did say, 'Don’t come here again, and don’t bring anything for me. Tell madam not to send any letters or messages through the boys.' He also said something else, but I can’t bring myself to say it... then he started crying."

"What did he say?" Nirmala urged.

Maid replied, "He said, 'My life is a curse.' And then he began crying again."

Nirmala let out a deep sigh, as if her heart was sinking. Her entire being seemed to cry out. She could not sit there any longer. She went to her room, lay down on the bed, and covered her face, sobbing uncontrollably.

"He knows now too," echoed in her heart over and over again. "He knows now too." Oh God, what will happen now? The fire of suspicion that had already been consuming her now blazed with even greater intensity. She had no concern for herself anymore. What hope was left for happiness in her life that she should desire it? She had tried to explain to herself that this was the penance for her past actions. Who could live shamelessly in such a state for long? She had sacrificed her entire life, all her desires, at the altar of duty. Her heart wept, but her face had to wear the color of a smile. She had to laugh and converse with the person whose mere sight repulsed her. The body whose touch felt as cold as a snake's, she had to embrace. Who could understand the revulsion and the pain she felt then? In those moments, she wished the earth would split open and swallow her whole.

But all the distress had remained confined to herself until now. She had let go of her own concerns, but the matter had now grown far more dire. She could not bear to see Mansaram's torment. Mansaram was a courageous, strong-willed young man, and she feared what this accusation would do to him. Her very soul shuddered at the thought of it. Regardless of how much suspicion surrounded her, even if it meant she had to take her own life, she could no longer remain silent. She had to protect Mansaram. She became desperate to do whatever it took, throwing away her hesitations and shame.

The lawyer always met her once before leaving for court after breakfast. The time for his visit had arrived. He should be coming soon, she thought, and Nirmala stood by the door waiting for him. But what was this? He seemed to be heading out already. The carriage was ready, and he was giving orders from outside. Was he not going to come in today? Was he planning to leave without seeing her? No, she wouldn't allow it.

She told Maid, "Go call Munshiji. Tell him there's something important, he must hear it."

Munshiji was just about to leave when he got the message. He came inside but did not come all the way to the room. Instead, he called from a distance, "What is it? Speak quickly; I have urgent work. I just received a letter from the headmaster that Mansaram has a fever. It would be better if we brought him home for treatment. So I will stop by there on my way to court. Do you have anything specific to say?"

To Nirmala, it felt like a thunderbolt had struck her. There was a fierce struggle between the rush of tears and her voice. Both were competing to come out first, neither willing to retreat. From the weakness of her voice and the strength of her tears, it was not difficult to tell which would win if the struggle continued another moment. Finally, both came out together, but as soon as they did, the stronger force took over. All that she managed to say was, "Nothing specific. You're going that way anyway."

Munshiji nodded, "I asked the boys; they said he was fine yesterday, just studying. I don't know what happened today."

Nirmala trembled with emotion, her voice shaking, "This is all your doing."

Munshiji frowned, "My doing? What have I done?"

"Ask your own heart," Nirmala shot back.

"I only thought he wasn't happy studying here, that maybe he'd do better with other boys around him. What's so wrong about that? What else have I done?"

Nirmala pressed on, "Think carefully. Was that really your only reason for sending him there? Was there nothing else in your mind?"

Munshiji hesitated, trying to mask his weakness by forcing a smile, "What else could there be? You tell me."

Nirmala sighed, "Alright, let it be. But please, bring him back today. I fear his illness will only worsen if he stays there. Sister-in-law can take much better care of him here than anyone else can."

She paused for a moment, then looked down, her voice trembling, "If you don't want to bring him back because of me, then send me away. I'll stay elsewhere comfortably."

Munshiji gave no response. He walked away, and a moment later, the carriage left for the school.

Oh mind, how mysterious, how complex is your nature. How swiftly you change your colors. Even a spinning firework takes a moment to shift its hues, but you—your changes are instant, far quicker. Where there was affection just moments ago, suspicion had now taken root again. He wondered, was she making excuses?

## Chapter - 10

*If you are expecting happy reunions and joyous moments, you may want to skip this story. This is not a tale of resolutions or peace; instead, it is a story drenched in misunderstandings, misplaced blame, and the silent cries of those who find themselves helpless in the face of fate. Here, we witness a tragedy that only deepens, with emotions spiraling into despair, and the innocence of pure hearts caught in the dark tides of suspicion. Brace yourself, for what lies ahead is neither uplifting nor comforting.*

Mansaram remained in deep worry for two days. The memories of his mother kept haunting him; he couldn't enjoy his food, nor could he focus on his studies. It seemed as if he had undergone a transformation. Two days passed, and even though he stayed at the boarding house, he couldn't complete the homework assigned by the school teachers. As a result, he had to stand on the bench—a punishment he had never faced before. The shame of this punishment weighed heavily on him.

On the third day, lost in his thoughts, he tried to console himself, "Am I the only one whose mother has died in this world? All stepmothers are like this. Nothing new is happening to me. Now, I should work doubly hard, like a man, and keep my parents happy, however they wish. If I earn a scholarship this year, I won't need to ask for anything from home. Many boys achieve great degrees on their own. Complaining about fate will do nothing."

Just then, Jiyaram arrived. Mansaram asked, "How is everything at home, Jiya? I suppose the new mother must be very happy?"

Jiyaram replied, "I don't know what's in her mind, but ever since you left, she hasn't eaten even one proper meal. She cries all the time. When father comes, she laughs, but otherwise, she is in tears. When you left, I also gathered my books to come and stay with you. But Maid went and told to new mother. Father was sitting there, and in front of him, new mother came, took my books, and cried out, 'If you too leave, then who will stay in this house? If it's because of me that you are all leaving the house, then fine, I will leave instead!' I angrily said, 'Why would you leave? It's your home, stay here comfortably. We are the outsiders. If we leave, you'll be at ease.'"

Mansaram praised, "You said well, very well." He continued, "She must have become even more upset and complained to father about it."

Jiyaram shook his head, "No, nothing like that happened. She sat on the floor and started crying. I felt pity and cried too. She wiped my tears with her dupatta and said, 'Jiya, I swear by God, I haven't uttered a word to your father about your brother. My fate is tainted, and I am living it.' And then she said more things, but I couldn't understand all of it—something about father."

Mansaram asked, concerned, "What did she say about father? Do you remember anything?"

Jiyaram hesitated, "I can't remember exactly. My memory isn't very good. But it seemed as if she had to pretend just to keep father happy. She said something about right and wrong, which I couldn't comprehend. But now I am sure—she never wanted you to come here."

Mansaram replied, "You don't understand these tactics; they are quite deep."

Jiyaram said, "Maybe you understand them, but I don't."

Mansaram retorted, "If you can't understand geometry, how can you understand such things? That night, when she called me for dinner, I was ready to come. But as soon as she saw father, she changed her tone completely—can I ever forget that?"

Jiyaram admitted, "That's the part I don't understand. Just yesterday, when I went home, she asked about you. I said you told me you would never step into that house again. I didn't lie; that's what you told me. As soon as I said that, she burst into tears. I regretted saying it. She kept saying, 'Will he leave the house because of me? Is he that angry with me? He left without even meeting me. I had made food for him, and he didn't come to eat.' What can I say? What trouble I am in. Then father came, and she quickly wiped her tears and smiled at him. This I just don't understand. She asked me to bring you back. I will pull you with me if needed. She's grown so thin in just two days—you would feel pity for her if you saw her. So, will you come?"

Mansaram didn't respond. His legs were trembling. Jiyaram left as soon as the attendance bell rang, but Mansaram lay on the bench, letting out a long sigh as if he hadn't taken a breath in ages. Words of unspeakable anguish escaped his lips: "Oh God." Besides the name of God, life felt utterly meaningless to him. This single sigh carried a depth of despair, emotion, compassion, and helpless plea—who could comprehend it all? He finally understood the truth, and his tormented heart cried out again and again, "Oh God, such an immense disgrace. Can there be a greater calamity in life? Can there be a greater disgrace in this world? Until now, has any father placed such a ruthless accusation on his own son? The one whom everyone praised for his character, who was an ideal for other young men, who never allowed impure thoughts near him—he is the one tainted with this worst disgrace."

Mansaram felt as though his heart would burst. The second bell rang, and the boys went back to their rooms, but Mansaram, resting his cheek on his palm, stared blankly at the ground, as if everything had sunk beneath the water, as if he could never show his face again. He didn't care about being marked absent or the fine—it didn't matter anymore. When his whole world had crumbled, what were these small matters? If he still survived despite this great disgrace, he would consider his life worthless.

In the intensity of that grief, he shouted, "Mother, where are you? Your son, whom you loved with all your heart, whom you considered the foundation of your life, is in grave distress today. The father who was supposed to protect him is holding a knife to his throat. Oh, Mother, where are you?"

Mansaram then began to ponder calmly, "Why is there suspicion on me? What is the reason for it? What could they have seen in me that led to this doubt? He is my father, not my enemy, who would lay such an accusation without any reason. Surely, he must have seen or heard something. He loved me so much—wouldn't eat without me. The idea that he could become my enemy is not without a cause. When did this suspicion first begin? The decision to place me in the boarding house came afterward. That night, when he came to my room to test me, I remember how his expression changed. What could have happened that upset him so much that day? I had gone to ask the new mother for something to eat, and father was there. Yes, now I remember—his face turned red right then. From that day, the new mother stopped studying by me. If I had known that going in and out of the house, talking to or tutoring mother, would make father angry, then I wouldn't have let this happen. And what must be happening to the new mother?"

Until now, Mansaram hadn't really thought of Nirmala. As soon as he did, his hair stood on end. "Oh, how will her tender, loving heart bear this blow? How deluded I was. I mistook her affection for cunning. I had no idea she had to act so harshly toward me just to dispel father's misunderstanding. Oh, how unfair I have been to her. She must be in worse shape than me. I came away here, but where can she go? Jiya said she hasn't eaten for two days and cries all the time. How can I make her understand? Why is she bearing this burden because of this wretched one? She keeps asking about me, keeps calling me back. How do I tell her, 'Mother, I have no complaint against you; my heart is clear towards you'? She must still be sitting and crying. What a great injustice. What has happened to father? Was this why he got married—to kill an innocent girl? Was she plucked only to be crushed? How will she be redeemed? How will her innocent face remain bright? She is being punished just for showing me kindness. Should I sit back and watch her endure such cruel blows? If not for my own dignity, then for her sake, I must sacrifice my life. There is no other way to save her. Oh, how many dreams I had—all of them must be turned to ashes. Doubting a pure woman, and all because of me. I must protect her with my life—that is my duty. That is true bravery. Mother, I will wash away this stain with my blood. That is the only salvation for both of us."

He remained lost in these thoughts the entire day. In the evening, his two younger brothers came to ask him to come home.

Siyaram said, "Why won't you come, my dear brother? Come on, please."

Mansaram replied, "I don't have the time to come just because you ask."

Jiyaram added, "After all, tomorrow is Sunday."

Mansaram retorted, "Even on Sunday, I have work."

Jiyaram insisted, "Alright, but you'll come tomorrow, won't you?"

Mansaram firmly said, "No, I have a match tomorrow."

Siyaram added playfully, "Mother is making mung laddoos. If you don't come, you won't get a single one. We will eat them all, and Jiya won't let you have any."

Jiyaram added, "Brother, if you don't come tomorrow, then maybe mother will come here herself."

Mansaram asked, "Really? Why would she do that? It would be troublesome if she came here. Tell her that I've gone somewhere to watch a match."

Jiyaram said, "Why would I lie? I'll tell her you were sulking. Just watch, I'll bring you back with me."

Siyaram chimed in, "We'll just tell her you didn't go to study today, that you lay around sleeping instead."

Mansaram promised them he would come tomorrow, just to get rid of them. When they left, he sank back into his worries. He spent the night turning from side to side, sleepless. Even the holiday passed with him just sitting around, filled with anxiety about whether mother might come after all. Any rattling of a carriage made his heart race. Could it be her?

The boarding house had a small dispensary where a doctor came for an hour in the evening. If any boy was ill, he would provide medicine. That evening, when the doctor arrived, Mansaram went over to him, deep in thought. The doctor knew Mansaram well, and upon seeing him, asked in surprise, "What has happened to you, young man? You look like you've wasted away. You haven't developed a bad habit, have you? What's the matter? Come here."

Mansaram smiled and said, "I have an illness called life. Do you have a cure for that?"

The doctor said, "I want to examine you. Your appearance has changed so much that you're hardly recognizable." With that, he took Mansaram's hand and examined his chest, back, eyes, and tongue, one by one. Afterward, he said with concern, "I will meet with your father today. It looks like you have phthisis. All the symptoms point to it."

Mansaram asked eagerly, "How long will it take to finish me off, doctor?"

The doctor scolded, "What kind of talk is this? I'll advise your father to send you to some hill station. God willing, you'll be well soon. The disease is still in its first stage."

Mansaram replied, "So it might still take a year or two. I can't wait that long. Listen, I don't have any phthisis or any other ailment. Don't put unnecessary worry in father's mind. I have a headache—give me something for it. Something that will help me sleep too. I haven't slept in two nights."

The doctor opened the cabinet containing poisonous medicines, took out a vial, and poured a little for Mansaram. Mansaram asked, "Is this poison? Would it kill someone if they drank it?"

The doctor replied, "No, it wouldn't kill, but it would make your head spin."

Mansaram asked again, "Is there anything here that would kill instantly?"

The doctor answered, "Not just one or two—there are many such medicines. This vial here—just one drop would be enough to end a life. Death would be instantaneous."

Mansaram asked, "Doctor, those who take poison—do they suffer much?"

The doctor explained, "Not all poisons cause suffering. Some make a person feel cold right away. This vial is one of those types. As soon as someone takes it, they lose consciousness and never wake up."

Mansaram thought, "Then dying is quite easy, so why are people so afraid of it? How could I get this vial? If I asked a chemist in the city for it, they'd never give it to me. Hmm, but getting it shouldn't be too difficult. At least I know that ending my life is easy."

Feeling like he had won a prize, a burden seemed to lift from Mansaram's heart. The storm cloud hanging over him had dispersed. After months, he felt a sense of relief. The boys were going to watch a theater performance and had gotten permission from the supervisor. Mansaram decided to join them. He felt so happy, as though there was no one more content in the world. He laughed so hard at the skits that he almost fell over. He was the first to clap and shout for encores. When songs played, he got excited and shouted, "Bravo!" repeatedly. The audience kept looking at him, and even the performers were curious to know who this enthusiastic person was. His friends were surprised at his exuberance. Normally, he was a calm and serious young man. Why was he so cheerful today? Why was there no end to his merriment?

Even when they returned at two in the morning, his laughter hadn't subsided. He overturned a boy's cot, locked several rooms from the outside, and laughed as he listened to the boys knocking from inside. Even the headmaster, who had been asleep, woke up at the noise and expressed his disappointment at Mansaram's mischief.

Who knew what kind of turmoil was raging inside him? The cruel blow of suspicion had crushed his dignity and self-respect. He no longer feared disgrace or insult. This wasn't mere amusement—it was the cry of his grieving soul.

When all the boys had finally gone to sleep, Mansaram lay down too, but sleep still eluded him. After a while, he sat up, packed his books, and put them away. If he was to die, then what was the use of studying? Life, filled with such obstacles and suffering, seemed worse than death. As these thoughts continued, dawn broke.

He hadn't slept even for a moment in three nights. He got up, but his legs were trembling, his head was spinning, his eyes burned, and his whole body felt weak. As the day went on, he didn't even have the strength to get up and wash his face. Suddenly, he saw Maid approaching with a servant carrying a cloth-wrapped bundle. His heart sank. Oh God, she has come! What will happen now? Maid couldn't have come alone—there must be a carriage waiting outside.

Mansaram, who could barely stand, suddenly ran towards her and asked in a trembling voice, "Has mother also come?"

When he learned that mother hadn't come, his heart calmed down. Maid said, "Brother, you didn't come yesterday, and madam kept waiting for you. Why are you upset with her? She says she hasn't complained about you at all. Today, she cried and asked me to bring you this sweet. She wants to know why you've left the house because of her. Where should I put this tray?"

Mansaram replied harshly, "Throw that tray on your head, witch. You've come all the way here with sweets. Don't you dare come here again. You brought a gift? Go back and tell her I don't need her sweets. Go tell her—it's your house, you stay there. They are having a good time, eating well, enjoying themselves. Go tell this to father, understood? I fear no one, and whatever they want to do, they can do. Let them try whatever they want, so they leave no regret."

Maid pleaded, "Brother, please take the sweet, otherwise she will die crying. Believe me, she'll die crying."

Mansaram suppressed the tears that were welling up, saying, "Let her die, I don't care. What happiness did she ever give me that I should regret? She ruined me completely. Tell her not to send me any messages—I don't need them."

Maid said, "Brother, you say you're eating well here, but your body has wasted away. You've become half the person you were when you came."

Mansaram said, "It's all in your eyes. Just wait; in a few days, I'll be as stout as an ox again. Tell her to stop crying. If I hear that she's crying or not eating, I'll be worse off for it. They've kicked me out of the house—fine, let them live in peace. She shows so much affection. I've read such tricks many times."

Maid left. As soon as she was gone, Mansaram felt a sense of coolness. Having to suppress his emotions for that performance had been unbearable for him. His self-respect was compelling him to end this deceitful behavior as soon as possible, but what would be the outcome? How would Nirmala bear this blow? Until now, whenever he imagined death, he hadn't thought of anyone else. But today, suddenly, he realized that another life was tied to his own. Would Nirmala think that her cruelty led to this? Wouldn't her tender heart break at that thought? Her life was still in jeopardy. Could this helpless woman, trapped in the harsh grip of suspicion, live long, seeing herself as a murderer? He covered himself with a quilt and lay down, but the cold was making his heart tremble. Shortly after, a high fever set in, and he lost consciousness.

In that state of unconsciousness, he saw many dreams. From time to time, he would jerk awake, open his eyes, and then drift back into unconsciousness. Suddenly, he heard munshiji's voice, and he woke with a start. Yes, it was father's voice. He threw off the quilt, got down from the cot, and stood. A surge of emotion rose in him—to die before his father, right then and there. He felt as though if he died, his father would truly be happy. Perhaps that's why he had come—to see how much longer it would take.

Munshiji took his hand, preventing him from falling, and asked, "How are you, son? Why didn't you stay in bed? Don't stand—lie down."

Mansaram replied, "I'm feeling perfectly fine. You didn't need to trouble yourself."

Munshiji didn't respond. Seeing his son's condition, tears welled up in his eyes. The robust child, who used to bring him so much joy, had now withered away to nothing. In just five or six days, Mansaram had grown so thin that it was hard to recognize him. Munshiji gently laid him back on the cot, covered him with the quilt, and began to think about what to do next. Would his son survive? The thought overwhelmed him with sorrow, and he sat on a stool, sobbing uncontrollably.

Mansaram too, lay under the quilt, weeping. Not too long ago, munshiji's heart would swell with pride at the sight of him, but today, seeing his son in such a wretched state, he pondered whether to take him home or not. Could he not receive treatment here? Munshiji thought, "I could stay here all day and night. The doctor is already here; there would be no difficulty." Taking him home seemed full of obstacles. The biggest concern was that Nirmala would sit by Mansaram's side all the time, and he wouldn't be able to stop her—that was unbearable for him.

Just then, the headmaster came and said, "I think you should take him with you. The carriage is here; there won't be any trouble. He will be better cared for at home."

Munshiji replied, "Yes, that's what I thought when I came, but his condition seems very fragile. A slight carelessness could lead to meningitis."

The headmaster insisted, "There might be a bit of inconvenience in taking him from here, but you know that the comfort he'll have at home can't be provided here. Besides, keeping a sick boy here is against the rules."

Munshiji said, "Shall I ask the principal for permission? I don't think taking him from here in this condition is appropriate."

Hearing the principal's name, the headmaster felt he was being threatened. He replied sharply, "The principal cannot break the rules. How can I take such a big responsibility?"

What now? Would he have to take him home? The excuse for not taking him was that moving him might worsen his condition. But taking him to the hospital after removing him from here—there was no excuse for that. Anyone who heard would say that to save the doctor's fees, they abandoned their son in a hospital. But now there was no choice but to take him. If the headmaster had been willing to take a bribe at that moment, he might have taken two or four years' salary. But where could rule-bound people have such wisdom or cunning? If someone had given Munshiji an excuse that would allow him not to take Mansaram home, he would have been forever grateful. There was no time to think further; the headmaster was like the devil riding his back. Helpless, Munshiji called the two servants and began to lift Mansaram.

In a semi-conscious state, Mansaram woke with a start and asked, "What is it? Who is it?"

Munshiji replied, "It's no one, son. I want to take you home. Come, let me lift you."

Mansaram protested, "Why are you taking me home? I don't want to go there."

Munshiji said, "You can't stay here; that's the rule."

Mansaram insisted, "No matter what, I won't go. Take me somewhere else—under a tree, in a hut—anywhere, but not home."

The headmaster told Munshiji, "Don't worry about what he says; he's not in his senses."

Mansaram shouted, "Who's not in his senses? Me? Am I abusing anyone? Biting anyone? Why am I not in my senses? Leave me here, whatever happens. Or take me to the hospital—I'll stay there. If I have to live, I'll live; if I have to die, I'll die. But I won't go home."

Hearing this insistence, Munshiji turned back to plead with the headmaster, but the headmaster was a man of rules—he wouldn't listen. If it was an infectious disease and it spread to another student, who would be responsible? This argument rendered Munshiji's legal arguments powerless. Finally, Munshiji said to Mansaram, "Son, why are you refusing to go home? You'll have all the comfort there."

Munshiji said this as if he were trying to convince Mansaram to go, but he secretly feared that Mansaram might actually agree. Munshiji was trying to find a way to take Mansaram to the hospital and place the responsibility on Mansaram himself. The headmaster was there as a witness—he could testify that Mansaram insisted on going to the hospital. Munshiji had no blame in this.

Mansaram, annoyed, said, "No, no, a hundred times no. I won't go home. Take me to the hospital, and tell everyone not to come see me. There's nothing wrong with me; I'm not sick. Leave me alone, I can walk by myself."

He stood up, walking unsteadily toward the door, but his legs gave way. If Munshiji hadn't caught him, he would have fallen badly. With the help of both servants, Munshiji brought him to the carriage and placed him inside. The carriage started toward the hospital.

That was exactly what Munshiji wanted. Despite his grief, he felt relieved. The boy was going to the hospital of his own will. Wasn't this proof that there was no affection for him at home? Didn't it show that Mansaram was innocent and he had wrongly suspected him? But soon, this satisfaction was replaced by a feeling of remorse. He was taking his beloved son to the hospital instead of home. There was no place for his son in his spacious house, even though his life was in danger. What irony!

A moment later, a thought suddenly struck Munshiji — had Mansaram perhaps sensed his feelings? Was that why he had grown to hate home? If so, it would be a catastrophe. The mere thought of such a disaster made Munshiji's hair stand on end and his heart pound. He felt a pang in his heart. If this fever was because of that, then God alone could save them.

Munshiji's condition at that moment was pitiful. The fire he had lit to warm his own cold hands was now burning his house. His heart, overwhelmed by compassion, sorrow, regret, and doubt, became restless. If the sound of his inner cries could have been heard, it would have made anyone weep. If his tears could have flowed, they would have formed a river. He looked at his son's colorless face with eyes full of fatherly affection, embraced him in his arms, and cried until he was breathless. The hospital gates were now visible in front of them.

# Chapter - 11

*If you wish to read a story filled with the blossoms of joy and the warmth of reunion, you should probably turn these pages and look elsewhere. Here lies not the promise of solace, but the weight of sorrow, a labyrinth of regret, and the tears that neither heal nor end. This chapter is a tale of shattered hearts and the silent battles of souls that struggle in vain to find light amid shadows.*

Munshi Totaram returned home from court in the evening, and Nirmala immediately asked, "Did you see him? How is he?"

Munshiji noticed that Nirmala's face bore no sign of worry or grief. In fact, her appearance was more adorned than usual. She rarely wore a necklace, but today one was around her neck. She had always loved her jhoomar, and today it shone brightly over her dark hair beneath her delicate silk sari, glowing like a chandelier's light.

Turning his face away, Munshiji said, "He's sick, what else can I say?"

Nirmala asked, "You went to bring him here, didn't you?"

Munshiji, irritated, replied, "He refused to come. Do you think I could have dragged him here by force? I tried to convince him, begged him to come home, assuring him that he would have no trouble there. But just hearing the word 'home' seemed to make his fever worse. He kept saying, 'I will die here, but I will not go home.' In the end, I had no choice but to leave him at the hospital. What else could I do?"

Rukmini, who had come and was standing in the verandah, spoke up, "He's stubborn by nature. He will not come here, and mark my words, he will not recover there either."

Munshiji said in a pleading voice, "If you could stay with him for a few days, sister, it would be such a relief. Please, sister, grant me this favor. Alone, he will cry himself to death. He keeps crying, 'Mother! Oh, Mother!' I am about to leave for the hospital; please come with me. His condition is not good. He doesn't even look like the same person anymore. Let's see what God wills."

Tears began to flow from Munshiji's eyes as he spoke, but Rukmini remained unmoved. She said, "I am ready to go. If my presence there can save my dear one's life, I will go running. But keep my words in mind, brother—he will not get better there. I know him well. He isn't ill; it's the pain of being cast out of his home. This grief has manifested as fever. You could use a thousand medicines, take him to the best doctors—even the civil surgeon—nothing will help him."

Munshiji said, "Sister, who has cast him out of the house? I only sent him there for his studies."

Rukmini replied, "Whatever your reason, he took it to heart. I am not in any position now; I have no right to speak. You are the master, and your wife is the mistress. I am merely a burden, a helpless widow living on your charity. Who will listen to me, who will care? But I cannot stay silent. Mansaram will only get better if he comes home, if your heart becomes what it once was." Saying this, Rukmini left. Her dim but experienced eyes could see the character of those in front of her clearly, and all her anger fell upon the innocent Nirmala. Even now, she stopped herself just short of saying, "As long as this madam remains in the house, its condition will continue to worsen." Though she didn't say it outright, her implication wasn't lost on Munshiji.

After she left, Munshiji lowered his head and began to reflect. He was so angry with himself at that moment that he felt like bashing his head against the wall and ending his life. Why had he married again? What need was there for marriage? God had given him not one but three sons. He was nearing fifty—why had he married? Was it God's plan to destroy him completely? He raised his head to look at Nirmala's smiling, calm figure, and then he left for the hospital. Nirmala's serene beauty had calmed his mind. After several days, he finally felt a sense of peace. Could a heart suffering from love truly be this calm and unmoved? No, never. The pain in one's heart cannot be hidden by mere expressions. He felt deeply ashamed of his unjust suspicions. His doubts about Mansaram also began to vanish, replaced now by a new worry. Had Mansaram figured it out? Was that why he refused to come home? If he had realized the truth, it would be a great disaster. The thought of such a calamity made Munshiji's heart tremble. It felt as if every bone in his body was aching to put out this inferno. He instructed the coachman to drive faster.

After many days, the heavy cloud that had overshadowed his heart seemed to dissipate, and waves of light were eager to burst forth. He leaned out to make sure the coachman wasn't dozing off. The horse's pace had never seemed so slow to him. When he reached the hospital, he rushed to Mansaram's side and saw that the doctor was standing there, deep in thought. Munshiji's hands and feet turned cold. He could barely speak, and in a shaky voice, he finally asked, "How is he, doctor?" Tears welled up, and when the doctor took a moment to respond, Munshiji felt as if his heart had stopped. He sat on the bed, took his unconscious son into his arms, and wept like a child. Mansaram's body was burning like a hot griddle.

Mansaram opened his eyes for a moment. Ah, what a terrifying yet piteous look it was. Munshiji clutched his son to his chest and asked the doctor, "How is he, doctor? Why are you silent?"

The doctor said in an uncertain voice, "You can see his condition for yourself. The fever is at 106 degrees, and what more can I say? The fever continues to rise. I'm doing everything I can, but it's in God's hands now. Since you left, I haven't moved from here for even a minute—I haven't even eaten. His condition is so critical that anything could happen at any moment. It's a severe fever, and he's completely delirious. Every now and then, he cries out, 'Mother, where are you?' Did someone say something to him at home?"

As the doctor was speaking, Mansaram suddenly sat up, pushed Munshiji off the bed, and in a frenzied voice shouted, "Why are you threatening me? Kill me! Go ahead, kill me now! If you don't have a sword, use a rope—I'll put it around my own neck. Oh, Mother, where are you?" Saying this, he fell unconscious again.

Munshiji stared at his son's limp form with pained eyes, then suddenly grabbed the doctor's hand and pleaded desperately, "Doctor, please save my son. For God's sake, save him, or I will be ruined. I'm not a wealthy man, but I will give you whatever you ask—just save him. Call the best doctors, consult with them, and I will bear all the expenses. I can't bear to see him like this. Oh, my precious son!"

The doctor said gently, "Sir, I swear I'm doing everything I can for him. If you want me to consult with other doctors, I will call Dr. Lahiri, Dr. Bhatia, and Dr. Mathur right now. I will also summon Vinayak Shastri. But I don't want to give you false hope—his condition is very serious."

Munshiji, sobbing, said, "No, doctor, don't say such words. Let my enemies be in such a critical condition, but not my son. God won't punish me like this. Send a telegram to doctors in Kolkata and Mumbai—I will serve you for the rest of my life. He is the light of my family, the foundation of my life. My heart is breaking. Please give him something to bring him back to consciousness. I just want to hear him speak, to know what's troubling him. Oh, my child!"

The doctor said, "Please calm yourself. You're an elder; crying and summoning an army of doctors won't help. Sit quietly, and I will call the city's doctors to see what they say. But you need to stay composed."

Munshiji said, "Alright, doctor, I won't say another word. I leave everything in your hands. Just do something so that he regains consciousness, so that he recognizes me and understands my words. Isn't there some kind of life-saving elixir? I just want to have a few words with him." Munshiji, overwhelmed, spoke directly to Mansaram, "Son, open your eyes. How are you feeling? I'm here, crying beside you. I have no complaint against you; my heart is clear towards you."

The doctor scolded, "There you go again, sir, talking nonsense. You're not a child; you're an elder—please show some patience."

Munshiji said, "Alright, doctor, I won't say anything more—it was my mistake. Do whatever you think is best. I've left everything to you. But is there no way for me to let him know that my heart is clear? Couldn't you say it for me, doctor? Tell him that his wretched father is sitting here, crying, that his heart is completely clear towards him. I had some doubts, but they have all been cleared. That's all I ask. I will sit quietly; I won't say a word. But please, just say that much."

The doctor said, "For God's sake, sir, have some patience, or I will have to ask you to leave. I'm going to the office to write to the doctors. Please stay quiet."

The cruel doctor! Seeing one's young son in such a state, what father could remain composed? Munshiji was a man of serious nature. He knew that crying out wouldn't help now, but staying quiet was impossible for him at this moment. If this illness had come about by fate, he might have been able to remain calm, comfort others, and call the doctors himself. But how could he stay composed, knowing that all this was his doing? Could any father be so heartless? Every fiber of his being was condemning him. He thought, why did I ever harbor such suspicions? Why did I imagine such terrible things without any proof? What should I have done in that situation? He couldn't decide. Truly, getting married again had been like striking his own feet with an axe. Yes, that was the root of all this trouble. But what I did wasn't unheard of. Everyone gets married, and their lives are filled with happiness. Isn't that why we marry, for happiness?

In this neighborhood, there were hundreds of men who had married twice, thrice, even up to seven times—many of them at a much older age than him. They lived comfortably until the end. It wasn't as if all their wives died first. Even those who married multiple times ended up widowed again. If everyone had gone through what I'm going through, who would ever think of marrying again? His own father had married at fifty-five, and Munshiji was sure his father had been at least sixty when he was born.

Yes, times had changed. In those days, women weren't educated. They considered their husbands worthy of worship, no matter what kind of men they were. Perhaps men back then acted shamelessly, ignoring everything. But if a young man can't be happy with an older woman, why should a young woman be happy with an older man? Still, I wasn't that old. Nobody would guess I was older than forty. But once youth fades, marrying a young woman does require some shamelessness—that's undeniable. Women, by nature, are modest. I'm not talking about immoral women, but most women are far more restrained than men. When they marry someone of their choice, they might flirt a little, but their hearts remain pure. When they marry someone they don't want, even if they never so much as glance at another man, their hearts are still troubled. A strong wall may resist everything, but a weak wall stands only as long as nobody pushes against it.

As Munshiji was lost in these thoughts, he dozed off. His emotions took shape in a dream. He saw his first wife standing in front of Mansaram, saying, "Husband, what have you done? The boy whom I nurtured with my own blood, you have treated so cruelly. You've put such a terrible stain on a child of such pure character. What are you waiting for now? You have lost him. I will take him away from your cruel hands. You were never so suspicious—did you marry only to embrace doubt? Such a brutal blow to a tender heart! Such a terrible slander! Those who live on, bearing such shame, must be heartless. My son cannot endure this!" Saying this, she took Mansaram in her arms and left.

Munshiji, crying, reached out to snatch Mansaram from her, and his eyes opened. There stood Dr. Lahiri, Dr. Bhatia, and half a dozen other doctors before him.

## Chapter - 12

*If you are searching for rays of joy amidst darkness, or hope blossoming without thorns, then perhaps this story will disappoint you. For this story is not one of triumphant love or serene conclusions. It is woven from shadows, regrets, and sacrifices that may make your heart ache. Here, despair mingles with love, misunderstanding battles truth, and every tender emotion walks hand in hand with pain. Only those with the courage to witness the rawness of human fragility may venture into these pages, for the solace you seek may just be a silent tear rolling down your cheek.*

Three days passed, and Munshiji did not return home. Rukmini visited the hospital twice a day to see Mansaram. The two younger boys also went to visit, but how could Nirmala go? It felt as if she had shackles around her feet. She was anxious to know about Mansaram's condition. When she tried asking Rukmini, she received taunts, and when she asked the boys, they gave vague answers. At times, her heart was restless, wanting to go see Mansaram herself.

She feared that suspicion might have weakened Munshiji's paternal love. Was his frugality perhaps hindering Mansaram's recovery? Doctors weren't kin; they cared only for their fees, indifferent to whether the patient ended up in heaven or hell. A powerful urge grew within her—she wanted to give the doctors a pouch of a thousand rupees and say, "Save him, and this pouch is yours." But she had neither the money nor the courage.

She thought that if she could be there, Mansaram might get better. He wasn't receiving the care he truly needed. Would his fever have lasted three days otherwise? This was no physical fever but a fever of the mind, and only with peace of mind could it subside. If she could stay by his side overnight, and if Munshiji did not hold any grudge, perhaps Mansaram might believe that his father's heart was clear, and he would soon recover. But would that happen? Could Munshiji be at peace seeing her there? Had his heart truly cleared? When leaving home, it had seemed as though he regretted his past mistakes.

For three days, Nirmala wavered in this dilemma. In the meantime, no cooking was done at home, nor did anyone eat. Pooris were bought from the market for the boys, while Rukmini and Nirmala went to bed hungry. They had no desire for food. On the fourth day, when Jiyaram returned from school, he stopped by the hospital before coming home. Nirmala asked, “Did you go to the hospital, son? How is he today? Has your brother improved?”

Jiyaram, on the verge of tears, replied, “Mother, today he wasn’t speaking at all. He was lying there silently, thrashing his hands and feet.”

Nirmala’s face went pale. Worried, she asked, “Was your father not there?”

Jiyaram said, “He was there. He was crying a lot today.”

Nirmala’s heart began to pound. “Were the doctors there?”

“Yes, the doctors were there, and they were discussing something amongst themselves. The chief civil surgeon said in English that they needed to put fresh blood into the patient. To that, Babuji said, ‘Take as much blood from me as you need.’ The civil surgeon laughed and said, ‘Your blood won’t do; we need blood from a young person.’ Then, he injected something into brother’s arm with a syringe. The needle was no less than four inches long, but brother didn’t even flinch. I was so scared that I closed my eyes.”

Great resolves are often born in moments of strong emotion. Nirmala, who was just moments ago trembling with fear, suddenly had her face glow with determination. She resolved to offer her own fresh blood. If her blood could save Mansaram’s life, she would gladly give every last drop. Let people think whatever they wished—she no longer cared.

She said to Jiyaram, “Run and get a carriage quickly. I’m going to the hospital.”

Jiyaram hesitated. “There must be a lot of people there right now. Why not wait until later?”

"No, go get a carriage now."

"What if father gets angry?"

"Let him be angry. Just bring the carriage."

Jiyaram said, "I'll tell him that mother insisted on it."

"Tell him."

While Jiyaram went to fetch a tonga, Nirmala combed her hair, tied it into a bun, changed her clothes, put on her jewelry, chewed a betel leaf, and stood at the door waiting for the tonga. Rukmini, sitting in her room, saw her preparations and asked, "Where are you going, dear?"

"I'm going to the hospital."

"What will you do there?"

"Nothing, what can I do? It's all in God's hands, but I wish to see him."

"I advise you not to go."

Nirmala replied humbly, "I'll come back soon, Sister. Jiyaram says his condition isn't good. I can't rest easy. Please come with me."

"I have already been there. Just know this—his life now depends on getting fresh blood. Who will give their blood, and why would they? There's a risk to life in that too."

"That's why I'm going. Wouldn't my blood suffice?"

"Of course it would. They need blood from a young person. But it would be better for your blood to be spilled into the river than to save Mansaram."

The tonga arrived. Nirmala and Jiyaram both got in, and the tonga set off. Rukmini stood at the door crying as she watched them leave. For the first time, she felt pity for Nirmala. If she could have, she would have tied Nirmala up to stop her. She could see where the surge of compassion and sympathy was leading her. Ah! This was the pull of misfortune, the road to ruin.

By the time Nirmala reached the hospital, the lamps had been lit. The doctors had already given their opinions and left. Mansaram's fever had subsided a bit, and he was staring blankly at the door. His gaze was fixed on the vast sky, as if he were waiting for some divine intervention. He was unaware of where he was or what condition he was in. Suddenly, upon seeing Nirmala, he sat up, startled. His trance broke. His lost consciousness seemed to return. He became aware of his surroundings and his condition, as though he had remembered something long forgotten.

He widened his eyes and looked at Nirmala, then turned his face away. Suddenly, Munshiji spoke sharply, "You! What are you doing here?"

Nirmala was speechless. How could she explain why she had come? Could there be any answer to such a straightforward question? What had she come for? Could such a simple fact—that a family member is unwell and she had come to see him—not be understood without asking? Why even ask? She stood there, stunned, as if she had lost her senses.

From what the two boys had told her about Munshiji's sorrow and regret, she had assumed that his heart had cleared. Now she realized that she had been mistaken—gravely mistaken. If she had known that even tears had failed to douse the fire of suspicion, she would never have come. She would have died pining at home, never setting foot outside.

Munshiji repeated his question, "Why have you come here?"

Nirmala answered fearlessly, "Why have you come here?"

Munshiji's nostrils flared. He angrily got up from the bed, grabbed Nirmala's hand, and said, "There is no need for you to be here. Come only when I call you. Understand?"

Oh, what a tragedy! Mansaram, who couldn't even move from his bed, stood up and, weeping, fell at Nirmala's feet. He cried, "Mother, you have troubled yourself for this wretch, and I shall never forget your kindness. I pray to God that in my next birth, I may be born from your womb, so that I may repay your debt. God knows I have never thought of you as a stepmother. I always saw you as my mother. You may not be much older than me, but to me, you were always in the place of my mother, and I always looked at you as such... I can't speak anymore, mother, forgive me! This is our final meeting."

Nirmala, holding back her tears, said, "Why do you talk like this? You'll be better in a few days."

Mansaram replied weakly, "I no longer wish to live, nor do I have the strength to speak." As he said this, he collapsed, exhausted, onto the ground.

Looking fearlessly at her husband, Nirmala asked, "What did the doctor say?"

Munshiji said, "They are all useless. They say he needs fresh blood."

"If fresh blood is found, can his life be saved?"

Munshiji looked at Nirmala sharply and said, "I am not God, nor do I consider the doctor to be God."

"Fresh blood isn't some unattainable thing."

"Neither are the stars in the sky unattainable, nor is death before us."

"I am ready to give my blood. Call the doctor."

Munshiji, astonished, said, "You?"

"Yes, why wouldn't my blood suffice?"

"You would give your blood? No, there's no need for your blood. There's a risk to your life."

Nirmala, with tearful eyes, said, "When else would my life be of any use?"

With moist eyes, Munshiji said, "No, Nirmala, your value has increased greatly in my eyes. Until today, you were merely a companion for my pleasure; from today, you are a subject of my devotion. I have wronged you greatly—please forgive me."

## Chapter - 13

*If you are looking for simple conclusions or a tale with cheerful resolutions, you might be disappointed with this story. Here, the story takes a turn into the raw depths of human sorrow and remorse. Like the fleeting moments of hope and love, what was once bright fades into uncertainty, and those who had once sought solace find themselves grappling with life's harshest truths. This is not a story of happy endings, but one of acceptance, courage, and the struggle to make sense of the inevitable.*

What was destined to happen, happened, and no one could stop it. The doctor was just about to extract blood from Nirmala's body when Mansaram, showing one final glimpse of his pure character, departed from this world of illusion. Perhaps, until that moment, his life had been waiting only for Nirmala. How could he leave without proving his innocence? Now his mission was complete. Munshiji now believed in Nirmala's innocence—but when? When the arrow had already left the bow, when the traveler had already placed his foot in the stirrup.

Life became a burden for Munshiji after the loss of his son. From that day onward, laughter never returned to his lips. Life now seemed empty. He still went to the courthouse, but not to argue cases—only to distract himself. After an hour or two, he would grow tired and leave. At the dining table, the food felt tasteless. No matter what Nirmala cooked, he could not eat more than a few bites; it seemed that each morsel stuck in his throat. Whenever he went to Mansaram's room, his heart shattered. The room that had once been illuminated by the light of his hopes now lay in darkness. He still had two sons, but when the milking cow dies, who can rely on the calves? When the blooming tree falls, what hope can there be from the saplings?

The sadness of losing a young son was profound. More painful still was the realization that he himself had taken his boy's life. Every time the thought crossed his mind, he felt as if his heart would burst—as if it would leap out of his chest.

Nirmala had true sympathy for her husband. She did everything she could to keep him content and never, even by mistake, brought up the past. Munshiji was embarrassed to discuss Mansaram with her. Sometimes, he had an intense desire to open his heart to her, to share all his emotions, but shame held him back. Thus, he did not even find the solace that comes from sharing one's pain, from letting others share in one's grief. The poison of unspoken pain continued to spread within him, and day by day, his body withered away.

Recently, Munshiji had grown closer to the doctor who had treated Mansaram. The doctor would come by occasionally to try to comfort him, sometimes even taking him out for a walk to get some fresh air. The doctor's wife, Sudha, had also visited Nirmala a few times, and Nirmala had been to their house as well. But whenever she returned from there, she remained sad for several days. Witnessing the happiness of the couple made her feel all the more sorrowful about her own condition. The doctor received only two hundred rupees a month, yet the two of them lived joyfully. They had only one maid, and Sudha herself had to do much of the household work. She wore very little jewelry, yet their love was such that wealth meant nothing to them. Seeing her husband made Sudha's face glow, and seeing her made her husband beam with happiness.

In comparison, Nirmala had far more wealth. Her body was adorned with jewelry, and she did not need to do any household chores herself. Despite all this wealth, Nirmala was unhappy, while Sudha, though less affluent, was content. Sudha had something that Nirmala lacked, something that made Nirmala's material riches feel insignificant. In fact, Nirmala even felt ashamed to wear her jewelry when visiting Sudha's house.

One day, after visiting Nirmala, Sudha noticed how sad she seemed and asked, "Sister, you seem very upset today. Is everything alright with the lawyer?"

"What can I say, Sudha? His condition is getting worse day by day. I don't know what fate has in store."

Sudha replied, "My husband says that he urgently needs to go somewhere with a different climate; otherwise, a serious illness could develop. He's told him several times, but the lawyer always says, 'I'm perfectly fine; I have no complaints.' Today, you should try telling him."

"If he didn't listen to the doctor, how will he listen to me?" Nirmala's eyes filled with tears. The fear that had haunted her heart for months could no longer stay buried. She said, "Sister, I don't see any good signs. Let's see what God decides."

Sudha comforted her, "You should urge him today to go somewhere for a change of climate. Spending two or three months away would help him forget many things. I also think that maybe even changing homes could lessen his grief. You won't be able to travel anywhere now, will you? What month is it?"

"The eighth month is passing. This is another worry that is tormenting me. I never prayed for this. Why has this trouble come upon me? I'm truly unfortunate, sister. My father passed away just a month before my wedding. As soon as he died, my fate changed. The family we were originally talking to about my marriage turned away. Poor mother had no choice but to get me married here. Now my younger sister's marriage is being arranged. Let's see where her fate leads her."

"Why did the other family back out of your wedding?"

"Who knows? Father was no longer alive, so who would give a bag of gold?"

"That's such cruelty. Where were they from?"

"Lucknow. I don't remember the name; he was a senior officer in the excise department."

Sudha's face grew serious as she asked, "And what did their son do?"

"He didn't do anything—he was studying. But he was very capable."

Sudha looked down and said, "Did he say anything to his father? He was young—couldn't he have stood up to his father?"

"How would I know, sister? Who wouldn't want a bag of gold? The priest who went with the proposal said that the boy himself refused. Only his mother tried to convince both father and son, but she didn't succeed."

"If I had met that boy, I would have given him a piece of my mind."

"What happened was written in my fate. Who knows what will happen to poor Krishna?"

That evening, when Dr. Sinha returned home, Sudha asked, "Tell me, what would you say about a man who, after arranging a marriage in one place, then turned away out of greed to marry somewhere else?"

Dr. Sinha looked at her curiously and said, "He shouldn't have done it, of course."

"Why don't you just say that it's vile behavior—an example of the worst kind of meanness!"

"Yes, I won't disagree with that."

"Whose fault is greater—the groom's or his father's?"

Dr. Sinha was still puzzled by Sudha's questions. He said, "It depends on the situation. If the groom is under his father's authority, then the father is at fault."

"Even if he's under his father's authority, doesn't a young man have any responsibilities of his own? If he needed a new coat, he'd plead and beg his father to get one, even against his wishes. Can't he raise his voice about something this important? You should say that both father and son are guilty, but the groom even more so. An old man thinks, 'I have to bear all the expenses, so let me get whatever I can from the bride's side.' But it's the groom's duty, if he's not completely sold out to selfishness, to show some integrity. If he doesn't do that, I'll say he's both greedy and cowardly. Unfortunately, that's exactly what my husband is, and I don't know in what words I should express my disdain for him!"

Dr. Sinha stammered, "That... that was a different matter. It wasn't about dowry. The girl's father had died. In such circumstances, what could we do? There was even talk that the girl had some defect. It was a different matter altogether. But who told you this story?"

"Go ahead, say that the girl was squint-eyed, or hunchbacked, or of questionable birth. Why leave anything out? Let me hear it—what defect did that girl have?"

"I didn't see her myself; I just heard there was some defect."

"The biggest defect was that her father died and she couldn't bring a large sum of money. Why are you ashamed to admit it? I won't bite your ears off! If I say a few harsh words, just let them go in one ear and out the other. If that girl had any defect, I'll say even goddess Lakshmi isn't without flaws. You made a mistake, that's all. And look where you ended up—with me."

"Who told you she was like that? Just like you believed what you heard..."

"I didn't just hear it—I saw her with my own eyes. No need to elaborate further, but I've never seen such a beautiful woman."

Dr. Sinha, startled, asked, "Is she here somewhere? Tell me the truth—where did you see her? Did she come to your house?"

"Yes, she came to my house, and not just once—she's come several times. I've also visited her several times. The lawyer's wife is the very girl you rejected for her supposed defects."

"Really?"

"Yes, absolutely. If she knew that you were the one, she might never step foot in this house again. Such a gentle, skilled, and exquisitely beautiful woman is rare even in this city. You always praise me, but I'm not even fit to be her servant. They have everything by God's grace, but when two people's hearts aren't in harmony, what does all the wealth mean? Her patience is remarkable—that she's enduring life with that old, irritable lawyer. If it were me, I'd have taken poison long ago. But just because she doesn't speak her pain doesn't mean it doesn't exist. She laughs, talks, wears jewelry, but every part of her cries in agony."

"Does she complain about the lawyer?"

"Why would she complain? Isn't he her husband? In this world, everything for her is tied to the lawyer. He may be old or sick, but he's her lord. Virtuous women don't complain about their husbands—that's the domain of the wicked. She suffers seeing his condition, but she never says a word."

"What possessed the lawyer to marry at such an age?"

"If men like that didn't exist, who would rescue poor maidens? You and your peers won't marry without extracting a heavy dowry, so where are these poor souls to go? You've committed a great injustice, and you'll have to atone for it. May God grant her husband a long life, but if something happens to him, her life will be ruined. Today she wept a lot. You men truly are heartless. I'll marry my Soham to a poor girl."

Dr. Sinha hadn't heard her last remark. He was deeply troubled. Again and again, the thought tormented him—what if something happened to the lawyer? Today, he saw the dreadful face of his selfishness. It was truly his fault. Had he insisted to his father that he would marry nowhere else, would his father have gone against his wishes?

Suddenly Sudha said, "Shall I arrange a meeting for you with Nirmala tomorrow? Let her see your face once. She won't say anything, but perhaps one glance from her will give you a scolding you'll never forget. Shall I arrange it tomorrow? I'll give a very brief introduction."

"No, Sudha, I beg you—don't do such a thing! I swear, if you do, I'll run away from home!"

"If you planted a thorn, why are you so afraid to reap its fruit? You plunged a dagger into someone's neck—watch them writhe a bit. My father gave you five thousand, didn't he? And soon you will get another five or six thousand for your younger brother's marriage. After that, there won't be anyone as wealthy as you in the world. Eleven thousand is a lot. My goodness—eleven thousand! It would take months to pile them up, and generations could live off it if the children began spending. Have you found any prospects yet?"

The teasing embarrassed Dr. Sinha so much that he couldn't even lift his head. All his wit and eloquence vanished. His face grew small, as if he had just been scolded. Just then, someone called for him from outside. He rushed out, relieved. Today, he truly understood how clever a woman's wit could be.

That night, as Dr. Sinha lay in bed, he said to Sudha, "Nirmala has a sister, doesn't she?"

"Yes, she mentioned her today. She's worried about her already. She said whatever was to happen to her happened, but now she's worried about her sister's future. The mother has nothing left. She'll probably have to marry her off to another old man."

"Can't Nirmala help her mother?"

Sudha's tone turned sharp. "Sometimes you talk utter nonsense. What can Nirmala do, other than give a few hundred rupees? Her husband is in this condition, and she has a long life ahead. Who knows what state her household is in? For the past six months, the poor lawyer has been homebound. Money doesn't rain from the sky. Even if they have ten or twenty thousand, it would be in the bank, not in Nirmala's hands. We get by on two hundred rupees a month; don't you think their expenses would be at least four hundred a month?"

Sudha fell asleep, but Dr. Sinha kept tossing and turning for a long time. Finally, he got up, sat at the desk, and began to write a letter.

# Chapter - 14

Two significant events happened simultaneously—Nirmala gave birth to a baby girl, Krishna's marriage was arranged, and Munshi Totaram's house was auctioned. The birth of the daughter was an ordinary event, though in Nirmala's eyes, it was the most important moment of her life. However, the other two events were extraordinary. How did Krishna's marriage get arranged in such a wealthy family? Her mother had no dowry to offer, and old Sinha, who had now retired and returned home, was well known for his greed. How did he agree to marry his son into such a poor family? It was hard for people to believe. Even more astonishing was the auctioning of Munshiji's house. If not a millionaire, people considered Munshiji a man of considerable means. How could his house be auctioned?

The truth was, Munshiji had borrowed some money from a moneylender to mortgage a village. He had hoped that in a year or so, he could repay the amount and, after some years, gain control of the land. The landowner would be unable to pay off the debt and interest, and this was what Munshiji had counted on. The village was large, yielding a profit of four to five hundred rupees annually, but Munshiji's hopes were dashed. Despite his best efforts, Munshiji could no longer go to court. The grief over losing his son had drained all his energy for work. Which father, with even an ounce of compassion, can find peace after taking his son's life? The moneylender had not received interest for a year and, despite repeated calls, Munshiji did not respond. Finally, the moneylender lost his patience and filed a lawsuit. Munshiji didn't even show up to defend himself, and suddenly, the decree was passed. Munshiji had no money at home to pay off the debt, and by this time, his reputation had also suffered. He could not make any financial arrangements, and the house was eventually put up for auction.

Nirmala, still in her confinement, heard the news and felt her heart sink. Despite having no other happiness in life, she was free from financial worries. Even if money is not the most important thing in human life, it is certainly close to it. Now, in addition to all her other deprivations, this concern also weighed on her. She sent word through the nurse, "Sell all my jewelry to save the house," but Munshiji refused to accept her proposal. From that day, Munshiji seemed even more weighed down by his worries. The wealth for which he had married was now merely a memory of the past. Out of remorse, he could no longer face Nirmala. He began to realize the injustice he had inflicted upon her.

On the twelfth day, after stepping out of confinement, Nirmala, carrying her newborn, went to her husband. Despite the difficult circumstances, she seemed as happy as if she had no worries at all. Holding her daughter close to her heart, she had forgotten all her troubles. Seeing the baby's bright and joyful eyes filled her heart with delight. In the expression of her motherhood, all her sorrows had disappeared. She wanted to place the baby in her husband's arms and feel his delight. But Munshiji recoiled at the sight of the girl. His heart did not swell with affection; he glanced at her with sorrowful eyes before bowing his head. The baby's face resembled Mansaram's completely.

Nirmala misunderstood his feelings. She drew the baby even closer to her chest, as if telling her, "If he cannot bear the weight of you, I won't let even his shadow fall on you from this day on. Doesn't his heart break as he disdains the precious gem I have attained with so much devotion?" She hugged the child tightly and returned to her room, crying for a long time. She made no effort to understand her husband's indifference; otherwise, she might not have thought him so cold.

Munshiji immediately realized his mistake. A mother's heart is so full of love that thoughts of future worries and obstacles do not frighten her. She feels within herself a superhuman strength that can overcome any challenge. Munshiji hurried into the house and, taking the baby in his arms, said, "She reminds me of Mansaram—exactly like him!"

Nirmala replied, "Sister-in-law also says the same."

Munshiji agreed, "She has the same big eyes and red lips. God has given me my Mansaram in this form. The same forehead, the same face, the same hands and feet! Lord, Your ways are unfathomable."

Suddenly, Rukmini entered. Seeing Munshiji, she said, "Look, Brother, doesn't she look like Mansaram? It's him! I won't believe anything else. This is Mansaram, plain and simple. It's only been a year since he left."

Munshiji replied, "Sister, each feature is a match. God has returned my Mansaram to me." (To the baby) "Why, little one, you are Mansaram, aren't you? Don't think of leaving me again; I'll drag you back if you do. How heartlessly you left! But haven't I brought you back? I tell you, don't ever think of leaving me again." Turning to Rukmini, he added, "Look, sister, how she's staring at me!"

At that very moment, Munshiji began to build his castle of hopes once again. Attachment pulled him back toward the world. Oh, human life! You are so fleeting, yet your dreams stretch so far. The same Totaram who had renounced the world and longed day and night for death was now fighting with all his might to reach the shore, clinging to the smallest straw. But who has ever reached the shore clinging only to a straw?

## Chapter - 15

Though Nirmala was preoccupied with her own household troubles, she could not resist going when she received news of Krishna's wedding. Her mother had earnestly requested her to come, and the most compelling reason was that Krishna's marriage was to take place in the same family where Nirmala's marriage had once been arranged. The most surprising part was how these people had agreed to marry without taking any dowry this time. Nirmala was deeply worried for Krishna, fearing that, like herself, Krishna would be pushed into an unsuitable match. She had hoped to support her mother in finding a proper groom for Krishna, but with her husband out of work and the moneylender's lawsuit, her own finances were strained. Given this, the news brought her a sense of relief, and she prepared to leave. Her husband accompanied her to the station. He was very attached to their young daughter and didn't want to part with her; he was even prepared to accompany Nirmala. However, going to her in-laws' place a month before the wedding didn't seem appropriate to Nirmala.

Until now, Nirmala had not shared her troubles with her mother. What was the point of lamenting over what had already happened and causing her mother more pain? Therefore, her mother believed Nirmala was living happily. But when she saw Nirmala's face, it felt as if her heart had been struck. Girls are not supposed to return from their in-laws' homes looking so worn, especially not a girl like Nirmala, who had been blessed with all the comforts of life. She had seen so many girls go to their in-laws' homes like the crescent moon and return like a full moon. In her mind, she imagined Nirmala's complexion would be glowing, her body filled out gracefully, her beauty enhanced. But now, seeing her, she looked half of what she used to be. The sparkle of youth was gone, and the charm that once captivated the heart was nowhere to be seen. The softness and beauty that come with a comfortable life had vanished. Her face looked pale, and her movements sluggish. Her mother asked, "Why, dear, weren't you getting enough to eat there? You were better off here. What trouble did you face?"

Krishna laughed and said, "She was the mistress there, wasn't she? A mistress always has countless worries. When is there time to eat?"

Nirmala said, "No, mother, the water there didn't suit me. I always felt heavy."

Mother: "Will your husband come for the wedding? I'll ask him why he took such a delicate girl and made her like this. Now tell me, why did you send money here? I never asked you for anything. I may be poor, but I have no intention of taking my daughter's money."

Nirmala, surprised, asked, "Who sent money, mother? I didn't."

Mother: "Don't lie! Didn't you send five hundred rupees in notes?"

Krishna: "If you didn't send them, then did they fall from the sky? Your name was clearly written on them, and the stamp was also from your place."

Nirmala: "I swear by your feet, mother, I didn't send the money. When did this happen?"

Mother: "About two or two and a half months ago. If you didn't send them, then where did they come from?"

Nirmala: "I have no idea, but I didn't send the money. Ever since our son passed away, my husband hasn't been going to the court, and my hands have been tied for money."

Mother: "This is really strange. You have no other close relative there, do you? Could your husband have sent it without telling you?"

Nirmala: "No, mother, I don't believe so."

Mother: "We must find out. I've already spent all the money on Krishna's jewelry and clothes. That's the real issue."

The two sisters talked late into the night. They discussed which girls from the neighborhood were married, who had children, whose wedding was celebrated with grandeur, who received the husband they had desired, and how much jewelry and gifts were received. Krishna wanted to ask about her sister's home several times, but Nirmala did not give her a chance. She knew that Krishna would ask questions that would be difficult for her to answer. Finally, Krishna asked, "Will your husband come to the wedding too?"

Nirmala: "He said he would."

Krishna: "Is he happy with you now, or is it still the same? I always heard that an older husband loves his wife dearly, but here it seems just the opposite. What's he angry about all the time?"

Nirmala: "How can I know what's in someone's heart?"

Krishna: "I think he might be upset with your coldness. You went there already bitter, and I suppose you said something there too."

Nirmala: "It's not that, Krishna. I swear, I have no ill feelings towards him. I serve him as much as I can. Even if he were a god, I couldn't do more. He loves me too. He constantly looks at me, but there is something beyond our control. What can he or I do about it? He cannot become young, and I cannot grow old. He takes numerous potions and tonics to stay young, and I've stopped consuming all rich foods in hopes that my leanness might reduce the apparent age difference. But neither do those substances work for him, nor do my sacrifices work for me. Since Mansaram's death, his condition has worsened."

Krishna: "Did you love Mansaram very much too?"

Nirmala: "He was such a boy that anyone who saw him loved him. I have never seen such big, soulful eyes in anyone. His face was always as bright as a lotus. He was so brave that if the occasion arose, he would jump into fire without hesitation. Krishna, when he would sit beside me, I would forget myself. I wanted him to always be in front of me, so I could just watch him. I swear there wasn't a trace of ill intention in my heart. If I ever even looked at him with any wrong feeling, let my eyes go blind. But I don't know why, seeing him beside me always made my heart swell with joy. That's why I pretended to need tutoring, otherwise, he wouldn't even come into the house. I know that if he had any impure intentions, I would have done anything for him."

Krishna: "Oh sister, stop. What are you saying?"

Nirmala: "Yes, it sounds bad to hear, and it is bad, but no one can change human nature. Just think, if you were married to a fifty-year-old man, what would you do?"

Krishna: "Sister, I'd take poison and end it all. I couldn't even look at his face."

Nirmala: "That's exactly it. That boy never once looked at me improperly, but old men are inherently suspicious. Your brother-in-law became his enemy and ended up taking his life. The day he learned that father suspected him of something regarding me, that very day he was struck with the fever that ended his life. The memory of that last moment never leaves my eyes. I went to the hospital. He was lying there unconscious from the fever, too weak to get up. But as soon as he heard my voice, he startled awake and cried, 'Mother, mother,' and fell at my feet. (Crying) Krishna, at that moment, I wanted to give him my life. He lost consciousness at my feet and never opened his eyes again. The doctor had suggested giving him fresh blood, and that's why I rushed there. But before the doctors could begin the procedure, his life ended."

Krishna: "Would his life have been saved with fresh blood?"

Nirmala: "Who knows? But I was ready to give every drop of my blood. Even in that state, his face shone like a lamp. If he hadn't rushed to my feet, if the blood had reached his body earlier, he might have survived."

Krishna: "Why didn't you make him lie down immediately?"

Nirmala: "Oh silly girl, you still don't understand. He fell at my feet, calling me mother, to clear his father's doubts about me. He stood up only for that reason. He gave his life to ease my pain, and his wish was fulfilled. Your brother-in-law has been straightforward ever since that day. Now I feel pity for him. The grief of losing a son will take his life. By doubting me, he has committed a grave injustice, and now he's paying the price. You'll be scared when you see him. He looks so old now, and his back is starting to bend."

Krishna: "Why are old men so suspicious, sister?"

Nirmala: "Ask them yourself."

Krishna: "I think they always have this feeling inside that they can't keep their young wives happy. That's why they get suspicious over small things."

Nirmala: "You already know the answer; why ask me?"

Krishna: "And that's why they act submissively to their wives. Outsiders think they love them a lot."

Nirmala: "Where did you learn all this in such a short time? Let it go and tell me, do you like your groom? You must have seen his picture?"

Krishna: "Yes, it came. Do you want me to bring it?"

In a moment, Krishna brought the photo and handed it to Nirmala. Nirmala smiled and said, "You're very fortunate."

Krishna: "Mother also liked him a lot."

Nirmala: "Do you like him or not? Don't just follow what others say."

Krishna, blushing: "He doesn't look bad, but God knows about his nature. Shastriji (priest motiram) said there are few young men as virtuous and well-mannered as him."

Nirmala: "Did they send your photo there too?"

Krishna: "Yes, Shastriji took it."

Nirmala: "Did he like it?"

Krishna: "How am I to know what's in someone's heart? Shastriji said he seemed pleased."

Nirmala: "Alright then, tell me, what should I give you as a wedding gift? Tell me now, so I can get it made."

Krishna: "Give whatever you want. He loves books a lot. You could get some good books for him."

Nirmala: "I'm not asking for him, I'm asking for you."

Krishna: "I told you, for myself."

Nirmala (looking at the picture): "All his clothes seem to be khadi."

Krishna: "Yes, he's a big admirer of khadi. I've heard he is good at giving speeches too."

Nirmala: "Then you will have to wear khadi too. But you always disliked coarse clothes."

Krishna: "If he likes coarse clothes, why would I dislike them? I've even learned how to spin yarn."

Nirmala: "Really? You can spin yarn now?"

Krishna: "Yes, sister, I can spin a little. Since he loves khadi so much, he must spin as well. If I don't know how to, I'd be embarrassed."

Talking like this, both sisters eventually fell asleep. Around two in the morning, Nirmala woke up to the sound of her baby crying and found Krishna's bed empty. Nirmala was surprised—where could Krishna have gone so late at night? She thought maybe she had gone to drink water, but the water jug was at the bedside, so where could she have gone? She called Krishna's name a few times, but there was no sign of her. Now Nirmala became anxious. Different thoughts started troubling her mind. Suddenly, she remembered that maybe Krishna had gone to her room. Once the baby was asleep, Nirmala got up and went to Krishna's room. Her guess was correct. Krishna was there, sitting at the spinning wheel, lost in her work. She probably hadn't even watched a theater show with such concentration. Nirmala was astonished. Entering the room, she said, "What are you doing, silly? Is this the time to spin yarn?"

Krishna, startled, got up, lowered her head in embarrassment, and said, "How did you wake up? I kept some water by your side."

Nirmala: "I ask you—don't you have time in the day, that you're sitting at the wheel late at night?"

Krishna: "There's no time during the day."

Nirmala (looking at the yarn): "The yarn is very fine."

Krishna: "Not at all, sister, this yarn is thick. I want to spin fine yarn to make a turban for him. That will be my gift."

Nirmala: "You've thought of a wonderful idea. What could be more valuable in his eyes than this? Alright, get up now; spin tomorrow. If you fall sick, everything will be ruined."

Krishna: "No, my dear sister, you go and sleep. I'll come soon."

Nirmala didn't insist further and went back to lie down. But she couldn't fall asleep. Seeing Krishna's enthusiasm and excitement stirred something deep within her. Oh, how happy her heart must be right now! Love had made her so eager. Then she remembered her own wedding. The day her engagement was finalized, all her cheerfulness and vitality seemed to vanish. Sitting in her room, she would cry over her fate and pray for her life to end. Like a criminal awaiting punishment, she had awaited the wedding—a wedding where all her desires would be crushed, and her hopes would be burned in the sacred fire under the wedding canopy.

## Chapter - 16

The month passed by quickly. The auspicious day of the wedding arrived, and the house was overflowing with guests. Munshi Totaram arrived a day before, accompanied by Nirmala's friend, Sudha. Though Nirmala had not insisted much, Sudha was eager to come herself. Nirmala's biggest curiosity was to finally meet the groom's elder brother and, if possible, thank him for his wisdom.

Sudha laughed and said, "Will you be able to talk to him?"

Nirmala: "Why not? What harm is there in talking? Now the relationship has completely changed. If I can't speak, then you are here."

Sudha: "No, sister, I can't do it. I don't talk to other men. Who knows what kind of a person he is?"

Nirmala: "He isn't a bad man. Besides, it's not as if you are marrying him; what harm can a little conversation do? If Doctor Sahab were here, I'd have made him give you permission."

Sudha: "Are those who are generous of heart also always good in character? Men hardly hesitate to ogle another's wife."

Nirmala: "Fine, don't talk. I'll do the talking. Let him stare as much as he can. Now, are you satisfied?"

Just then, Krishna came in and sat down.

Nirmala smiled and asked, "Tell me the truth, Krishna, why do you seem restless right now?"

Krishna: "Brother-in-law is calling you. Go see what he wants. You can have your chats later. He's really upset."

Nirmala: "What is it? Didn't you ask him?"

Krishna: "He seems unwell. He's grown very thin."

Nirmala: "Then why didn't you sit with him for a while to comfort him? Why did you come running here? Just thank God that you didn't get a husband like that. Go sit and chat with him for a bit. Old men have such charming conversation. Young men aren't so boastful."

Krishna: "No, sister, you go. I can't sit there."

When Nirmala left, Sudha asked Krishna, "The wedding procession must have arrived by now. Why hasn't the welcoming ritual begun yet?"

Krishna: "I don't know, sister. Shastriji is gathering the necessary items."

Sudha: "I heard that the groom's sister-in-law has quite a harsh nature."

Krishna: "How do you know?"

Sudha: "I heard it, so I'm warning you. You might have to bear a few harsh words."

Krishna: "I'm not one to pick fights. If they have no complaints against me, why would they start trouble for no reason?"

Sudha: "Yes, that's what I heard. She picks fights for no reason."

Krishna: "I believe in one thing—humility can melt even the hardest hearts."

Suddenly, a commotion broke out—"The wedding procession is arriving!" Both women rushed to the window. Within a moment, Nirmala also arrived. She was eager to catch a glimpse of the groom's elder brother.

Sudha said, "How will we know who the elder brother is?"

Nirmala: "I could ask Shastriji. That man on the elephant must be Krishna's father-in-law. Oh, look, how did Doctor Sahab get here? Isn't that him on the horse?"

Sudha: "Yes, it's him."

Nirmala: "They must be friends with those people. There's no family relation, is there?"

Sudha: "If we get a chance to meet, I'll ask. I don't know."

Nirmala: "The gentleman in the palanquin doesn't seem like the groom's brother."

Sudha: "Definitely not. He looks rather stout."

Nirmala: "I can't figure out who's on the other elephant."

Sudha: "Whoever it is, it's not the groom's brother. Look at his age—he must be over forty."

Nirmala: "Shastriji is busy with the welcoming ceremony right now, otherwise, I'd ask him."

Just then, the barber arrived. The keys to the trunks were with Nirmala, and they needed some money for the ceremony, so her mother had sent him. This was the same barber who had gone with Pandit Motiram in tilak ceremony.

Nirmala asked, "Do you need the money now?"

Barber: "Yes, sister, please come give it to me."

Nirmala: "Alright, I'm coming. But tell me first, do you recognize the groom's elder brother?"

Barber: "Of course I do. There he is, right in front."

Nirmala: "Where? I don't see him."

Barber: "There, on the horse. That's him."

Nirmala, astonished, said, "What are you saying? The one on the horse is the groom's brother? Are you sure or just guessing?"

Barber: "Sister, how could I forget? I just delivered the refreshments."

Nirmala: "Oh, that's Doctor Sahab. He lives next door to me."

Barber: "Yes, yes, that's Doctor Sahab."
Nirmala looked at Sudha and said, "Did you hear this, sister?"
Sudha tried to hold back her laughter, "He's lying."

Barber: "Alright, alright, I'm lying. I won't argue with elders. But shall I ask Shastriji to confirm it?"
When the barber took too long, Motiram himself came into the courtyard, shouting, "It seems like it's in God's hands to maintain the honor of this house. The barber came an hour ago, and we still haven't got the money."

Nirmala called out, "Come here, Shastriji. How much money do you need? I'll get it out."

Grumbling and panting loudly, Shastriji came upstairs and said with a deep sigh, "What is it? This isn't the time for chit-chat. Quickly, get the money out."

Nirmala: "Alright, I'm getting it. Do I have to fall on my face to do it? But tell me first, who is the groom's elder brother?"

Shastriji: "Ram, Ram, you've kept me hanging for such a small matter. Couldn't the barber tell you?"

Nirmala: "The barber said it's the one on the horse."

Shastriji: "Well, who else could it be? He's right."

Barber: "I've been saying that for ages, but sister here wouldn't believe me."

Nirmala looked at Sudha with a mix of affection, teasing, and mock anger, and said, "So, you've been playing your tricks on me all this time! If I'd known, I wouldn't have called you here. My goodness, you're a sly one! You've been plotting this for months, and never once let it slip. I'd have blurted it out in just a few days."

Sudha: "If you'd known, would you have come to my place at all?"

Nirmala: "Oh my, I've talked to Doctor Sahab several times! All this blame will be on your head. Look, Krishna, see how mischievous your sister-in-law is! Be wary of her."

Krishna: "I'll wash this goddess's feet and place them on my head. How lucky I am to meet her!"

Nirmala: "I understand now. You must have been the one to send the money too. If you nod now, I swear I'll hit you."

Sudha: "One doesn't insult a guest invited to their home."

Nirmala: "Let's see how much news I can dig up about you. I wrote a little note to maintain your honor, and you actually came. What do the people there say about it?"

Sudha: "I told everyone before coming."

Nirmala: "I'll never come to your house again. You could've at least hinted for me to keep a distance from Doctor Sahab."

Sudha: "What harm is there in him seeing you? If he hadn't, how would he regret what he lost? Now, seeing you, he clenches his fists. He can't say anything, but he regrets his mistake in his heart."

Nirmala: "I'm never coming to your house again."

Sudha: "Now you won't be able to escape me. I'll find a way to come to your house too."

The welcoming ceremony was over. The guests were sitting and having refreshments. Munshiji was sitting beside Doctor Sinha. Nirmala saw them through the screen from the balcony, and her heart skipped a beat. One was a picture of health, youth, and radiance, while the other... it was better not to say anything. Nirmala had seen Doctor Sahab countless times before, but today, the thoughts that came to her mind were unlike anything she had felt before. Again and again, she felt like calling him over and scolding him, taunting him until he remembered it forever, making him cry, but she let it go out of mercy.

The wedding procession had moved to the guesthouse. The preparations for the meal were underway. Nirmala was busy arranging the food trays when suddenly, a maid came and said, "Miss, Sudha Rani is calling you. She's in your room."

Nirmala left the trays and hurried to see Sudha. But as soon as she stepped inside, she froze—Doctor Sinha was there.

Sudha smiled and said, "Here, sister, I called him over. Scold him as much as you want. I'm guarding the door, he can't run away."

Doctor Sahab, in a serious tone, said, "Who is running away? I stand here with my head bowed."

Nirmala folded her hands and said, "May you always show such grace, and never forget. This is my humble request."

## Chapter - 17

*If you are drawn to tales where darkness is softened by a silver lining, where hope shines unbroken, you might find yourself uneasy as you turn these pages. For in this tale, life is laid bare with all its ruthlessness—where the heartaches do not transform into blessings, and the pain is not erased by a stroke of fortune. This story is not one of triumphant conclusions but of human resilience against the relentless tides of fate.*

After Krishna's marriage, Sudha left, but Nirmala stayed at her maternal home. Munshiji wrote to her multiple times, but she did not return. She didn't feel like going back; there was nothing there that attracted her. Here, she spent her days happily serving her mother and looking after her younger brothers. Had Munshiji come to get her, perhaps she would have agreed to go back, but the mischief the neighborhood girls had played during the wedding made him reluctant to come. Sudha wrote several letters, but Nirmala made excuses to her as well. Finally, one day, Sudha brought a servant along and arrived herself. Once they embraced, Sudha said, "It seems like you're afraid of going back there."

Nirmala replied, "Yes, sister, I am afraid. I've come here after three years, and now I feel like I might stay forever. Who will come to bring me back?"

Sudha reassured her, "Come anytime you feel like it. Munshiji is very anxious at home."

Nirmala smiled. "Very anxious, I'm sure. He probably loses sleep at night."

Sudha frowned, "Sister, your heart is like stone. Looking at his condition, one feels pity. He says there's no one at home to talk to—no son, no daughter. Whom should he share his thoughts with? Ever since they moved to the new house, he has been very sad."

"But God has given him two sons," Nirmala responded.

Sudha sighed, "He complains a lot about them. Jiyaram doesn't listen to him at all and talks back rudely. And the younger one follows Jiyaram's lead. Poor man often weeps remembering Mansaram."

Nirmala's face grew serious. "Jiyaram wasn't mischievous before; when did he become so troublesome? He used to obey everything I said without question."

"Who knows, sister? He's said some terrible things—accusing his father of poisoning his brother and calling him a murderer. He's taunted him many times for marrying you. One day, he even picked up a stone to hit him."

Nirmala was deeply troubled. "This boy has become quite dangerous. Who told him his father poisoned his brother?"

"You'll have to ask him yourself," Sudha replied.

A new concern arose in Nirmala's mind. If Jiya behaved like this with his father, how would he treat her? Late into the night, she remained absorbed in these thoughts. Memories of Mansaram flooded her mind. Life would have been peaceful with him. If Jiya treated his father this way, how would she fare after her husband's death? The house was already gone, there was likely still some debt, and their income was uncertain. Only God could save them.

For the first time, Nirmala began to worry about her child. What would become of this poor little one? The Lord had brought this trouble upon her, but she had no need for it. If this girl was to be born, she should have been born into a fortunate household. The little one was sleeping, clinging to her chest. Nirmala held her even tighter, as if someone was about to take her away.

Sudha's bed was next to Nirmala's. Nirmala was drowning in a sea of worries, while Sudha enjoyed her sweet sleep. Did she ever worry about her child? Death does not distinguish between young and old, so why didn't Sudha fear the future? Nirmala had never seen her anxious about anything.

Suddenly, Sudha woke up. Seeing that Nirmala was still awake, she asked, "Are you still not asleep?"

"I just can't sleep," Nirmala replied.

"Just close your eyes, and sleep will come. As soon as I get on the bed, I feel as if I've died. Even if I wake up, I hardly realize it. I don't know why I sleep so much. Maybe it's some kind of illness."

"Yes, a very serious illness," Nirmala teased. "It's called the disease of comfort. Tell Dr. Sinha to start treatment."

"And what should I think about when awake? Sometimes, memories of home keep me awake, but only then," Sudha said.

"And you never think of Dr. Sinha?"

"Never. Why should I? I know he's probably come back from playing tennis, eaten, and is now resting comfortably."

Nirmala smiled, "Look, even Soham is awake now. If you wake up, how could he keep sleeping?"

Sudha chuckled, "Yes, sister, it's strange. He wakes up with me and sleeps with me. He must be a hermit from his past life. See the mark on his forehead? There are similar marks on his arms. He must have been a hermit."

"Hermits don't wear sandalwood tilak marks. He must have been a cunning priest," Nirmala teased. "Tell me, Soham, where were you a priest?"

Sudha laughed, "I'll have him marry your daughter."

"Oh, stop it, sister! How can a brother marry his own sister?"

"I will do it, no matter what anyone says. Where else would I find such a beautiful daughter-in-law? Look, sister, doesn't he feel a little warm to you? Or is it just my imagination?"

Nirmala touched Soham's forehead. "No, no. He has a fever. When did it come? He's still drinking milk, right?"

Sudha looked worried, "He was fine when he fell asleep. Maybe he caught a chill; I'll cover him up. He should be fine by morning."

But by morning, Soham's condition had worsened. His nose was running, his fever was higher, his eyes had reddened, and his head drooped. He wasn't moving or smiling—just lying still, seemingly annoyed by any sound. He had also begun to cough. Now Sudha was really worried. Nirmala suggested calling Dr. Sinha, but her elderly mother intervened, "There's no need for a doctor here. I can see clearly—it's the evil eye. What can a doctor do?"

"Mother, who could give him the evil eye? He hasn't even been outside," Sudha protested.

"No one gives it intentionally, dear. Sometimes even parents' gazes can affect the child. He hasn't cried once since he came here. Cheerful children often meet such a fate. When I saw him playing so happily, I feared something bad would happen. Look at his eyes—don't they seem glassy? That's a sure sign of the evil eye."

The elderly maid and the neighbor's wife both agreed. Soon Mahangu came, looked at Soham, and laughed, "Mistress, it's surely the evil eye. Bring some thin sticks. If God wills, the boy will be laughing by evening."

Five reeds were brought, and Mahangu tied them together, muttered something, and ran the bundle over Soham's head five times. When he checked the sticks afterward, they were of different lengths. All the women gasped in amazement. How could anyone doubt it was the evil eye now? Mahangu repeated the ritual, and this time the sticks came out nearly equal, showing that the effect of the evil eye was almost gone. Assured, Mahangu promised to return in the evening and left.

But Soham's condition continued to deteriorate throughout the day. His coughing got worse, and by evening, despite Mahangu's rituals showing improvement, Soham coughed all night. His eyes rolled back several times. Sudha and Nirmala stayed up the entire night. They were relieved when morning came, but now Sudha's mother suggested another solution—a religious ritual from a cleric.

The maid wrapped Soham in a shawl and took him to the mosque to get blessed. Even though the ritual was repeated in the evening, Soham didn't get better. That night, Sudha decided to send a telegram to her husband if Soham's condition remained the same. But before midnight, Soham passed away. Sudha's greatest treasure slipped from her hands in an instant. Only two days ago, they had been joking about his marriage, and today he had left everyone in tears. The innocent face that had filled his mother's heart with joy now tore it apart with grief.

Everyone tried to console Sudha, but her tears wouldn't stop. She couldn't bear the thought of facing her husband. He didn't even know his son had been ill. A telegram was sent that very night, and the next morning, by nine o'clock, Dr. Sinha arrived in his car. When Sudha heard he had arrived, she burst into tears again.

After Soham's last rites, Dr. Sinha came inside several times, but Sudha didn't go to him. How could she face him? What would she say? She felt she had taken away the most precious thing from his life and thrown it into the river. Her heart shattered at the thought of facing her husband, whose eyes used to light up seeing Soham in her arms. When Soham crawled into his father's lap, he refused to leave, even when Sudha called him back. Now, whom would she take to her husband? Seeing her empty arms, wouldn't he break down in tears? She felt she'd rather die than face him. She clung to Nirmala, afraid she might run into him.

"Sister, what's done is done. How long will you keep avoiding him? He's leaving tonight," Nirmala urged.
Sudha, tears filling her eyes, said, "How can I face him? I'm afraid my legs will give way the moment I see him, and I'll collapse."

"I'll go with you," Nirmala assured her. "I'll hold you."
"Promise you won't leave me," Sudha whispered.

"I won't," Nirmala replied.

Sudha's heart overflowed with sorrow. Despite this terrible calamity, she was still sitting, and that astonished her. Soham had been so deeply loved by Dr. Sinha. Who knew what he must be feeling? What could she say to console him? She would end up crying herself. "Is he really leaving tonight?" she asked.

"Yes," Nirmala confirmed, "Mother said he hasn't taken leave."

The two friends walked toward the men's room, but at the room's door, Sudha asked Nirmala to leave her alone.

Dr. Sinha concerned about what Sudha must be feeling. His mind was plagued with all sorts of doubts and fears. He was ready to leave but found himself unable to move. Life seemed empty. He thought, "If God was going to take away such a precious gift so soon, why did He give it at all?" He had never prayed for a child. He could have lived childless, but now, having had a child and then losing him felt unbearable. Was man really just a toy in God's hands? Was this the purpose of human life? Just like children's sandcastles—built for no reason, and destroyed just as easily? But even children have affection for their sandcastles, their paper boats, their wooden horses. They protect their best toys with all their might. If God were like a child, He would surely be a strange one. But reason doesn't accept God as this capricious child. The creator of the boundless universe couldn't be a mere reckless player. We attribute to Him qualities far beyond our understanding. Playfulness is not one of those great virtues! How could taking the lives of innocent children be considered a game? Would God engage in such a cruel pastime?

Suddenly, Sudha entered the room quietly. Dr. Sinha approached her, saying, "Where were you, Sudha? I've been waiting for you."

To Sudha, the entire room seemed to blur through her tears. She put her arms around her husband's neck and rested her head on his chest, crying. But in this outpouring of tears, she found immense patience and comfort. Clinging to her husband's chest, she felt a strange energy and strength flowing into her—as though a flickering candle had found shelter from the wind. Dr. Sinha gently took her tear-streaked face in his hands and said, "Sudha, why are you so broken-hearted? Soham came to do what he had to in this life, and then he left. Just as a tree grows with water and sunlight but becomes strong only against powerful winds, love too grows through the trials of suffering. Many

will laugh with us in joy, but only a true friend will weep with us in sorrow. Today, Soham's death has united us completely. Today we have seen each other's true selves."
Sudha, still sobbing, said, "I thought it was an evil eye. Oh! You didn't even get to see his face one last time. I don't know where he found the understanding he had in his last days. Whenever he saw me cry, he would forget his own pain and smile. By the third day, his little eyes closed, and I couldn't even give him proper medicare." As she spoke, her tears welled up again.

Dr. Sinha embraced her and said in a trembling voice, "Beloved, has there ever been a child or elder whose family could completely fulfill the wish for treatment and care? It is always left incomplete."

Sudha wiped her tears, "Nirmala helped me a lot. I could catch a few naps, but she never closed her eyes. She stayed up all night, carrying him or comforting him. I will never forget her kindness. Are you leaving today?"

Dr. Sinha replied, "Yes, I couldn't take leave. The civil surgeon is out on a hunting trip."
Sudha sighed, "They're always out hunting, aren't they?"
"What else do kings do?" Dr. Sinha said with a faint smile.
Sudha's voice was resolute, "I won't let you go today."
"My heart doesn't want to leave either," Dr. Sinha admitted.
"Then don't go—send a telegram. I will come back with you. I'll bring Nirmala too."
When Sudha returned, her heart felt lighter. Her husband's tender and loving words had taken away all her grief and sorrow. Love has boundless faith, boundless patience, and boundless strength.

## Chapter - 18

When a great misfortune befalls us, it doesn't just bring sorrow but also exposes us to the taunts of others. Society finds it the perfect opportunity to comment, something it's always eager to do. When Mansaram died, it seemed as if the entire community had found a reason to gossip about Munshiji's household. No one knew the inner truth; what was evident was that it was all the doing of a stepmother. Everywhere people talked—may no child ever have to face a stepmother! A woman who destroys her own settled home, who is ready to wield the knife at the neck of her dear children, is the one who marries again despite already having kids. There's never been a case where a stepmother did not ruin the family. The same father who once adored his children becomes their enemy the moment a new wife arrives. His whole mindset changes. Never has there been a goddess who considered her stepchildren her own.

The worst part was that people weren't satisfied with just gossiping. There were also a few who suddenly became very sympathetic toward Jiyaram and Siyaram. They expressed their solidarity with the boys, and a couple of women even remembered the virtues of their late mother and shed tears. "Alas! Poor woman, she never knew that her beloved children would face such a fate after her death! Do they even get proper milk and butter now?"

Jiyaram would respond, "Why wouldn't we?"

But the women would say, "Oh, you get it, do you? Getting it can mean different things, dear. Someone may bring cheap, watered-down milk and leave it there—drink it if you want or leave it, who cares? Your poor mother used to have it freshly milked. The face says it all, and yours says it's not the same."

Jiyaram, who barely remembered the taste of the milk his mother gave him or what he looked like during those days, had no reply. He stayed silent.

It was natural that these well-wishers' comments began to have an impact. Jiyaram grew increasingly resentful of his family. After Munshiji's house was auctioned off and they moved into a rented one, Nirmala had to cut back on expenses. They were no longer earning as before, so how could they spend freely? The two servants were let go. Jiyaram resented these cutbacks. When Nirmala went to her maternal home, Munshiji even stopped providing milk. The burden of the newborn daughter had already begun to weigh on his mind.

Siyaram, angered, said, "Is cutting the milk supposed to build a palace for us? Why not stop the food too!"

Munshiji replied, "If you like milk so much, why don't you go bring milk yourself? I can't afford water at the cost of milk."

"How can I go out and bring milk myself? What if a schoolmate sees me?" Jiyaram protested.

Munshiji shrugged. "Just tell them it's for yourself. It's not stealing."

"It's not stealing? And what if someone sees you getting the milk? Won't you be ashamed?" Jiyaram snapped.

"Not at all. These hands have drawn water from wells and carried sacks of grain. My father wasn't a millionaire," Munshiji replied.

"My father wasn't poor, so why should I bring milk of my own?" Jiyaram countered. "Why did you dismiss the servants anyway?"

"Can't you figure out that my income isn't what it used to be? You're not that ignorant," Munshiji shot back.

"And why is your income reduced?" Jiyaram persisted.

Munshiji sighed. "When you lack understanding, what's the point in explaining? I'm tired of life, son. Who has the energy to take on cases anymore? My heart isn't in it. I'm just living out my days now. All my dreams died with Mansaram."

"By your own hand," Jiyaram muttered.

Munshiji shouted, "You fool! It was God's will. Who would willingly cut their own throat?"

"God didn't tell you to get remarried," Jiyaram retorted.

Munshiji couldn't contain himself any longer. His eyes blazed with anger as he said, "Are you trying to pick a fight today? On what grounds? You're not the one providing for me! When you're capable, come and preach to me. Right now, you have no right to lecture me. Learn some respect and decency first. You are not my advisor, and I don't need your permission for what I do with my money. It's my hard-earned wealth, and I'll spend it as I see fit. You don't even have the right to speak. If you disrespect me again, there will be serious consequences. When I didn't die after losing a precious son like Mansaram, do you think I'd die without you? Understand that!"

Despite the harsh scolding, Jiyaram didn't back down. He said fearlessly, "So you want me to stay silent no matter how much suffering we go through? I can't do that. I won't follow the path that earned my brother respect and cost him his life. I'm not brave enough to take poison and die. I bow out from such so-called respect."

"Do you not feel ashamed talking like this?" Munshiji asked.

"Children imitate their elders," Jiyaram replied.

Munshiji's anger faded. He realized his outburst would have no effect on Jiyaram. He got up and went for a walk. Today, he felt he had received the message that this household was heading for ruin. From that day on, there was almost daily friction between father and son. Munshiji tried to bear it, but Jiyaram grew bolder. One day, Jiyaram even told Rukmini, "I spare him only because he's my father. Otherwise, I have friends who, if I wanted, could beat him up in broad daylight."

Rukmini relayed this to Munshiji. Outwardly, he appeared indifferent, but fear gripped his heart. He stopped taking evening walks and was reluctant to bring Nirmala back, fearing that the troublemaker would treat her the same way. Jiyaram had once muttered under his breath, "Let's see how she enters this house now."

Munshiji knew well that he couldn't do anything. If it had been an outsider, he could have involved the police and law. But what could he do to his own son? It's true—people are defeated by their own children.

One day, Dr. Sinha called Jiyaram over to talk to him. Jiyaram respected the doctor, so he sat quietly and listened. When Dr. Sinha finally asked, "What do you really want?" Jiyaram replied, "Should I speak plainly? You won't be offended?"

"No, go ahead. Say what's on your mind," Dr. Sinha assured him.

"Well then, ever since my brother died, I get angry just looking at my father's face. I feel as though he killed my brother, and one day he'll kill us too. If that wasn't his intention, why did he remarry?" Jiyaram said.

Dr. Sinha barely managed to hold back a smile. "Why would he need to get married just to kill you both? I don't understand that. Couldn't he have done it without marrying again?"

"Never. Back then, his heart was different. He loved us more than his life. Now he doesn't even want to look at us. His only wish is that no one remains in the house except him and those two," Jiyaram replied, his voice trembling. "They want us out of the way now. They want to make our lives miserable so we'll leave. That's why he doesn't take on cases anymore. If both of us brothers were to die today, just watch how happy they'd be."

"If he wanted you gone, couldn't he have falsely accused you and thrown you out?" Dr. Sinha asked.

"I'm ready for that, anytime," Jiyaram said defiantly.

"And how have you prepared?" Dr. Sinha asked.

"When the time comes, you'll see," Jiyaram said and walked away. Dr. Sinha called him several times, but Jiyaram didn't look back.

A few days later, Dr. Sinha met Jiyaram again. Dr. Sinha loved going to the cinema, and Jiyaram was just as passionate about films. Dr. Sinha started discussing movies with Jiyaram, drew him into conversation, and eventually invited him to his home. It was dinner time, so they both ate together. Jiyaram enjoyed the meal very much. He remarked, "Ever since the cook left, the joy of eating at our place has disappeared. Auntie insists on strict vegetarian food. I eat it reluctantly, but I don't look forward to it."

Dr. Sinha smiled, "When food is cooked in my house, it's usually quite flavorful. I suppose your aunt avoids onions and garlic?"

"Yes, sir, she even refuses to touch it. Father doesn't care whether anyone eats or not. That's why the cook left. If we have no money, where do the jewels come from?" Jiyaram said bitterly.

"That's not it, Jiyaram. His income really has reduced a lot. You trouble him a great deal," Dr. Sinha said kindly.

Jiyaram laughed, "Me? Trouble him? I swear I never talk to him. He's made it his mission to slander me. He harasses me without reason. He even dislikes my friends. How can anyone live without friends? I'm not a rogue who keeps bad company, but he picks on me because of my friends. Yesterday, I told him straight—my friends will come to the house, whether he likes it or not. Sir, no one can tolerate constant bullying."

Dr. Sinha shook his head, "Honestly, I feel sorry for him. This should have been his time to rest. He's old, grieving the loss of a grown son, and his health isn't good. What can someone like that do? Whatever little he manages, it's already more than enough. If you can't do anything else, at least try to make him happy through your behavior. It's not that hard to please the elderly. Believe me, a kind word, a smile—it's enough. How much does it cost you to ask, 'Father, how are you feeling?' He feels deeply hurt seeing your rebelliousness. He's cried in front of me more than once. He admits he made a mistake by remarrying, but why are you neglecting your duty? He's your father—you should serve him. Don't say anything that would hurt him. Why give him the opportunity to think that everyone enjoys his earnings but no one cares about him? I'm much older than you, Jiyaram, but to this day, I've never talked back to my father. Even now, if he scolds me, I just bow my head and listen. I know he says everything for my own good. Who could be a greater well-wisher than parents? Who can ever repay their debt?"

Jiyaram wept silently. Not all of his good intentions had vanished yet, and he saw his own wickedness clearly. He hadn't felt such remorse in a long time. Crying, he said to Dr. Sinha, "I'm very ashamed. I was misled by others. From now on, you won't hear a single complaint about me. Please ask my father to forgive me. I really am most unfortunate. I've troubled him a lot. Tell him to forgive my mistakes; otherwise, I will blacken my face and go away somewhere. I'll drown myself."

Dr. Sinha was overjoyed at his own success in persuading Jiyaram. He hugged him and sent him home. It was eleven o'clock when Jiyaram got home. Munshiji had just stepped outside after dinner. As soon as he saw Jiyaram, he said, "Do you know what time it is? It's almost midnight."

Jiyaram replied humbly, "I ran into Dr. Sinha and went to his house with him. He insisted I stay for dinner, so I had to. That's why I'm late."

"Did you go to complain to Dr. Sinha, or was there something else?" Munshiji retorted.

Jiyaram felt a portion of his humility fading. "Complaining is not my habit," he said.

"Not at all—you have no tongue in your mouth. I suppose those who tell me about you are lying?" Munshiji said coldly.

"I can't speak for other times, but today at Dr. Sinha's, I said nothing I wouldn't repeat in front of you right now," Jiyaram said.

"How wonderful," Munshiji said sarcastically. "Very pleased to hear it. Have you taken initiation from a guru today?"

Another portion of Jiyaram's humility vanished. He raised his head and said, "A man can be ashamed of his faults and improve without needing initiation. One doesn't need a guru to change."

"Will your good-for-nothing friends stop coming over now?" Munshiji asked.

"Why do you call them that unless you have proof?" Jiyaram replied.

"All your friends are scoundrels. There's not a decent one among them. I've told you many times not to bring them here, but you never listened. Today, I'm telling you for the last time—if you gather those ruffians here again, I'll involve the police."

Jiyaram's remaining humility evaporated. He retorted, "Fine, go ahead and call the police. Let's see what they do. Most of my friends are sons of police officers themselves. If you're set on fixing me, why should I avoid the trouble?"

Jiyaram then left for his room, and soon the sound of harmonium music filled the air. The flame of gentleness that had been lit within him had been extinguished by cruel sarcasm. The stubborn horse, coaxed into moving, had bolted again, now refusing to budge and instead pushing back against the cart.

## Chapter - 19

This time, Nirmala had to return with Sudha. She had wanted to stay longer at her maternal home, but how could the grieving Sudha remain alone? In the end, Nirmala had no choice but to come back. Rukmini said to Maid, "Look how radiant the sister-in-law looks after returning from her maternal home!"

Maid replied, "Sister, a mother's cooking always tastes best to her daughter."

Rukmini nodded, "You're right, Only a mother knows how to truly feed her child."

Nirmala felt as though no one at home was happy about her return. Munshiji showed much affection, but he could not hide the worries weighing on his heart. The baby girl had been named Asha by Sudha—a fitting name, as she seemed to embody hope itself. Just seeing her dispelled all anxieties. When Munshiji tried to hold her, she began to cry and clung to her mother, as though she didn't recognize him. Munshiji tried to win her over with sweets, but there was no servant in the house to fetch them, so he asked Siyaram to bring two annas worth of sweets from the market.

Jiyaram was also sitting nearby and spoke up, "We never get sweets."

Annoyed, Munshiji replied, "You're not a child anymore."

"What are we then, old men? If you buy some sweets for us, maybe we'll find out whether we're children or old," Jiyaram said sarcastically. "Hand over one rupee. Let's see if Asha can awaken our luck too."

"I don't have the money right now," Munshiji said, handing coins to Siyaram. "Go, and hurry."

Jiyaram intervened, "Siyaram won't go. He's nobody's servant. If Asha is her father's daughter, then he's his father's son too."

Munshiji frowned. "Why are you talking nonsense? Aren't you ashamed of comparing yourself to a little girl? Go, Siyaram, take this money."

But Jiyaram snapped, "Don't go, Siya! You're not anyone's servant."

Siyaram was caught in a dilemma—whose word should he follow? Ultimately, he chose to follow Jiyaram. At worst, his father would scold him, but Jiya might beat him up, and then whom would he complain to? "I'm not going," he declared.

Angrily, Munshiji threatened, "Fine, but don't come to me asking for anything again."

Munshiji himself went to the market and returned with a rupee's worth of sweets. He felt embarrassed to ask for only fifty paisa' worth—the sweet vendor knew him, and what would he think? Munshiji brought the sweets inside, and when Siyaram saw the large bowl of sweets, he regretted not obeying his father. Now, how could he face everyone and take the sweets? He knew he had made a mistake. He began comparing the blows he received from Jiyaram to the sweetness of the sweets.

Suddenly, maid brought two plates of sweets and set them down in front of the boys. Jiyaram scowled, "Take it away!"

"Why are you angry, babu? Don't you like sweets?" maid asked.

"The sweets are for Asha, not for us. Take them away, or I'll throw them out onto the street. We beg for every penny, and here a whole rupee's worth of sweets comes in," Jiyaram retorted bitterly.

"Take it, Siyaram. If he doesn't want it, then you have it," maid said.

Siyaram hesitated, but as soon as he reached for the sweets, Jiyaram yelled, "Don't touch them, or I'll break your hand! Greedy!"

Terrified by the scolding, Siyaram backed away, unable to bring himself to take the sweets. When Nirmala heard about all of this, she went to calm the two boys, but Munshiji stopped her.

"You don't understand," Nirmala said to him. "All this anger is directed at me."

"He's become insolent," Munshiji said. "I've held back only because I don't want people to say I'm mistreating my children without a mother. Otherwise, I'd have put an end to his insolence in no time."

"That's exactly what I fear—what people will say," Nirmala admitted.

"I won't worry about that anymore. Let people say what they want," Munshiji declared.

"They weren't like this before," Nirmala said sadly.

"Well, he has the audacity to tell me, 'Why did you marry again when your children were already here?' And he doesn't even hesitate to say we poisoned Mansaram. He's no son; he's an enemy," Munshiji said with a mix of anger and pain.

Jiyaram had been eavesdropping near the doorway, curious about what the couple would say about the sweets. But when he heard Munshiji's final words, he couldn't hold back. "If I weren't an enemy, then why would you be after me like this? I figured out your intentions long ago. My brother was naïve and got fooled, but your tricks won't work on me. Everyone says you poisoned him. Why do you get angry when I say it?"

Nirmala was stunned, as if hot coals had been thrown onto her body. Munshiji tried to silence Jiyaram by scolding him, but Jiyaram stood his ground, returning every blow with a stronger one. Even Nirmala grew angry at him. This young boy, who neither worked nor contributed to the family, was standing there acting as if he was the one taking care of everyone. She glared at him, "Enough, Jiyaram. We get it; you're very capable. Now go sit outside."

Munshiji had been somewhat restrained in his words until now, but emboldened by Nirmala's support, he grew more aggressive. Grinding his teeth, he lunged forward, and before Nirmala could stop him, he slapped Jiyaram. The blow landed on Nirmala instead, making her fall back. Her head spun; she hadn't imagined Munshiji's frail hands had such strength. Holding her head, she sat down.

Munshiji's anger flared even more, and he swung his fist again. But this time, Jiyaram caught his hand, pushed him back, and said, "Talk from a distance, or you'll only humiliate yourself for no reason. I'm holding back out of respect for mother, otherwise, I'd show you!" With that, he stormed out.

Munshiji stood there, stunned. At that moment, if a divine thunderbolt had struck Jiyaram, Munshiji might have felt true satisfaction. The same son whom he had once cherished in his arms was now the source of countless vile thoughts running through his mind.

Rukmini had been in her room until then. She now came out and said, "Once a son grows up, one shouldn't raise a hand against him."

Biting his lip, Munshiji said, "I will throw him out of this house. Let him beg or steal—I don't care."

"Whose reputation will suffer then?" Rukmini questioned.

"I don't care about that," Munshiji replied curtly.

Nirmala sighed, "Had I known my return would cause this storm, I wouldn't have come back, not even by mistake. It's better if I leave now; I can't stay in this house any longer."

Rukmini tried to console her, "He respects you a lot, sister-in-law. Otherwise, something even worse might have happened today."

"What more could happen, Didi? I tread as carefully as I can, yet I'm still blamed. I haven't even been back in this house for long, and look at what's already happened. May God bring peace," Nirmala said, feeling a deep sense of despair.

That night, no one came to dinner except Munshiji, who ate alone. Nirmala was left with a new anxiety—how would life move forward now? If it was only about her own survival, she wouldn't worry much. But now, an additional burden had been placed on her shoulders. She wondered, "What fate awaits my little daughter, God?"

## Chapter - 20

*If you are seeking a tale of bright joy and comforting endings, I urge you to close this book and seek another. This tale will lead you through the twisted paths of agony, where hope dangles like a fragile flower beneath stormy skies, and where love and despair intermingle in a dance as ancient as time. Here, you will not find easy resolutions or simple comforts; instead, you'll witness hearts breaking under the weight of fate, as courage rises and falls amidst relentless trials. Prepare yourself, for this story may leave you with more questions than answers and a sadness that no words could fully mend.*

How could one sleep when burdened by worries? Nirmala tossed and turned on her cot, wishing for sleep to come, but it seemed as if sleep had vowed to stay away. She had put out the lamp, opened the window shutters, and even moved the ticking clock to another room, yet sleep eluded her. She had thought over everything she needed to, reached the end of her worries, but her eyelids refused to close. Finally, she lit the lamp again and began reading a book. She had barely read two or three pages when she felt herself dozing off, the book lying open beside her.

Suddenly, Jiyaram entered the room. His legs were trembling. He looked around the room, up and down. Nirmala was asleep, and on the shelf beside her head, there was a small brass box. Jiyaram tiptoed over, slowly took the box down, and quickly slipped out of the room. Just at that moment, Nirmala's eyes opened. Startled, she sat up, moving toward the door. Her heart skipped a beat. Was that Jiyaram? What was he doing in my room? Could I have been mistaken? Maybe he had come from Didi's room? What would he be doing here? Perhaps he had something to tell me, but at this hour, what could it be? What were his intentions? Her heart quivered.

Munshiji was sleeping upstairs on the terrace. Without a parapet, Nirmala could not sleep there. She thought of waking him up but lacked the courage. He was a suspicious man; who knew what he might think or how he might react? She went back and began reading her book again. She would find out in the morning when she could ask. Maybe she was mistaken; sometimes sleep plays tricks on the mind. But even with this decision, she could not fall asleep.

In the morning, she herself went to Jiyaram, carrying his breakfast. He was startled to see her; usually, maid brought it—why was she here today? He couldn't muster the courage to meet her eyes. Nirmala looked at him with trusting eyes and asked, "Did you come into my room last night?"

Feigning surprise, Jiyaram said, "Me? Why would I go there at night? Did someone go in?"

Nirmala, in a tone suggesting she fully believed his answer, said, "Yes, I thought someone left my room. I didn't see his face, but from the back, it looked like it could have been you. How could we find out who it was? Someone was there for sure—of that, there's no doubt."

Jiyaram tried to prove his innocence, saying, "I went to watch a play last night. I stayed at a friend's house afterward. I only just returned. There were several friends with me; you can ask them. Honestly, I'm really scared. What if something's gone missing and I get blamed for it? No one catches the real thief, and I'll be the one held responsible. You know how father is—he'd come after me to beat me up."

Nirmala replied, "Why would your name come up? Even if you were there, no one could accuse you of theft. Theft is done with someone else's belongings, and you can't steal your own things."

So far, Nirmala hadn't even looked at her box. She began preparing food. After Munshiji left for the court, she decided to go visit Sudha. It had been several days since they'd met, and she needed to discuss last night's incident as well. She said to maid, "Bring me the jewelry box from the room."

Maid returned and said, "There's no box there. Where did you keep it?"

Nirmala said, irritated, "Can't you do anything right the first time? Where else would it be? Did you check the cupboard?"

Maid replied, "No, madam, I didn't check the cupboard. Why would I lie?"

Nirmala smiled and said, "Go look again, quickly."

In a moment, Maid returned empty-handed, "It's not in the cupboard either. Tell me where else to look."

Nirmala got up, annoyed, saying, "I don't know why God gave you eyes! Watch, I'll find it myself from the same room."

Maid followed her into the room. Nirmala looked at the shelf, opened the cupboard, peeked under the cot, and then opened the large trunk of clothes. There was no sign of the box. She was surprised—where could it have gone?

Suddenly, the events of the previous night flashed before her eyes like lightning. Her heart skipped a beat. Until now, she had been calmly searching, but now her anxiety rose. She began searching frantically, but still found nothing. She looked where she should have, and where she shouldn't have. How could such a big box hide under the bedding? But she still checked under the bedding. With each moment, her face grew paler, and her heart felt like it was sinking. Finally, in despair, she pounded her chest and began to cry.

Jewelry is a woman's only possession. She has no right over any other property of her husband's. It is her strength, her pride. Nirmala had jewelry worth five or six thousand rupees. Whenever she wore it and went out, her heart would swell with joy for that time. Each piece of jewelry felt like a shield against adversity. Just last night, she had thought she would not let herself become Jiyaram's servant. God forbid she ever had to beg from anyone. She would use this jewelry to sustain herself and ensure a future for her child. What was there to worry about? No one could take it from her. Today, it was her adornment, and tomorrow, it would be her support. The thought had given her so much comfort! And now, that security was gone. She was without support, without any pillar to lean on in the world. The foundation of her hopes had been cut off, and she wept bitterly.

"Oh God! Was it too much for you to see me have even this? You already left me crippled, and now you've blinded me too. Who will I turn to now, whose door will I beg at?"

Sweat drenched her body, and her eyes were swollen from crying. Nirmala sat with her head down, sobbing. Rukmini was trying to console her, but her tears wouldn't stop, and the fire of grief wouldn't cool.

At three o'clock, Jiyaram returned from school. On hearing he had come back, Nirmala, in a half-crazed state, rushed to his room and said, "Jiya, if it was a joke, then please give it back. What will you gain by tormenting a wretched person?"

For a moment, Jiyaram felt a pang of guilt. This was his first attempt at theft, and he hadn't yet developed the cruelty that finds amusement in violence. If he had the box now, and if there was still a chance to return it to the shelf, perhaps he wouldn't have let the opportunity go. But the box was no longer with him; his friends had taken it to the jeweler and sold it for a pittance. For a thief, there is no protection but lies.

"Mother," he said, "why would I do such a thing to you? You're still doubting me. I've already said I wasn't home last night, but you just won't believe me. It's very upsetting that you think I'm so low."

Nirmala wiped her tears and said, "I don't doubt you, Jiya. I don't think you stole anything. I just thought maybe it was a prank."

How could Nirmala accuse Jiyaram of theft? The world would say that because the boy's mother was dead, they were accusing him of stealing. It would be her reputation that would be tarnished.

Jiyaram, trying to reassure her, said, "Come, let me look around and see who might have taken it, or where the thief could have come from."

Maid said, "Jiya, you talk about the thief coming in. Thieves can slip in like mice; there are windows all around here."

Jiyaram asked, "Did you search everywhere properly?"

Nirmala replied, "The whole house has been searched. Where else do you want me to look?"

Jiyaram retorted, "You people sleep like the dead."

At four o'clock, Munshiji came home. Seeing Nirmala's condition, he asked, "How are you feeling? Is there any pain anywhere?" He said this as he lifted Asha into his arms. Nirmala couldn't respond and began to cry again.

Maid said, "Nothing like this has ever happened before. My entire life has been spent in this house, and never before has even a penny gone missing. Now the world will say it's maid's doing—God alone will save my honor."

Munshiji was undoing the buttons of his coat but paused, rebuttoning them as he asked, "What happened? Was something stolen?"

Maid replied, "All of madam's jewelry is gone."

Munshiji asked, "Where was it kept?"

Nirmala, through her sobs, narrated the entire incident of the previous night, except she didn't mention seeing Jiyaram leaving her room.

Munshiji sighed deeply, saying, "God is so unjust. It seems the unfortunate ones are always the ones to be struck. It feels like bad times have truly arrived. But how did the thief get in? There are no signs of forced entry, no broken locks or windows. I've never done anything to deserve such a punishment. I kept saying not to leave the jewelry box on the shelf, but who listens?"

Nirmala replied, "How was I to know this calamity would strike?"

Munshiji responded, "You should have known that good times don't last forever. If I were to get it remade today, it would cost no less than ten thousand rupees. Given our current situation, which you're well aware of, we can barely cover expenses—how will we afford new jewelry? I'm going to the police station to report it, but don't expect much."

Nirmala, concerned, objected, "If you know nothing will come of reporting it, then why are you going?"

Munshiji said, "How can I not go? Such a big loss can't just be ignored."

Nirmala added, "If we were meant to have it, it wouldn't have gone missing. If it's not in our fate, then how could we have kept it?"

Munshiji replied, "If it's in our fate, it'll return; if not, then it's already gone."

Munshiji left the room, but Nirmala caught his hand and said, "I'm telling you, don't go. What if we end up paying a bigger price?"

Munshiji pulled his hand away, saying, "You're being stubborn like a child. Losing ten thousand isn't something I can easily accept. I may not be crying, but only I know what I'm feeling inside. This loss has struck me to the core."

Munshiji could say no more; his throat closed up. He quickly left the room and headed to the police station.

The inspector at the station held Munshiji in high regard; Munshiji had once gotten him acquitted from a bribery case. He accompanied Munshiji back for the investigation. His name was Alayar Khan. Evening had set in.

The inspector examined the front and back of the house, carefully inspected Nirmala's room, checked the terrace, spoke discreetly to a few people from the neighborhood, and then told Munshiji, "Sir, I swear to God, this isn't the work of an outsider. I swear, if it turns out to be someone from outside, I will give up my job as an inspector. Is there any servant in your house you suspect?"

Munshiji replied, "There's only one maid in the house nowadays."

The inspector said, "Oh, she's harmless. This is the work of someone cunning, I swear."

Munshiji asked, "Then who else could it be from inside the house? I have two sons, a wife, and a sister here. Who should I suspect?"

The inspector replied, "I swear to God, it's the work of someone from inside, whoever it may be. God willing, I'll have news for you in two or four days. I can't promise all the jewelry will be recovered, but I swear I'll catch the thief."

After the inspector left, Munshiji came to Nirmala and told her what he had said. Nirmala felt a chill run through her. "Tell the inspector to stop the investigation; I beg you," she said.

Munshiji asked, "But why?"

Nirmala replied, "Why should I explain now? He says it's someone from inside the house."

Munshiji said, "Let him say whatever he wants."

Jiyaram sat in his room, praying, his face pale with fear. He had heard that the police could read a person's guilt from their face. He didn't have the courage to go outside. He was desperate to know what the men were discussing. As soon as the inspector left and maid came out for some chore, Jiyaram asked, "What was the inspector doing?"

Maid came closer and said, "The bearded inspector says it's someone from inside the house; there's no one from outside."

Jiyaram asked, "Did father say anything?"

Maid replied, "No, he didn't say anything—just kept mumbling 'hmm, hmm.' There's only one maid in the house who's not family; everyone else is."

Jiyaram said, "I'm an outsider too, just like you."

Maid protested, "Why would you be an outsider?"

Jiyaram replied, "Did father tell the inspector he doesn't suspect anyone in the house?"

Maid said, "I didn't hear him say anything like that. The inspector even said, 'Maid is just a fool; how could she steal?' Munshiji seemed ready to accuse me, though."

Jiyaram sighed, "So, you're off the hook. It's only me left. Tell me, did you see me at home that day?"

Maid said, "No, Jiya, you went to watch the play."

Jiyaram asked, "Will you testify to that?"

Maid replied, "What are you saying? madam will have the investigation stopped."

Jiyaram said, surprised, "Really?"

Maid nodded, "Yes, She keeps telling them not to investigate. Let the jewelry go, but father won't listen."

For five or six days, Jiyaram barely ate. Sometimes he managed a few bites, other times he would say he wasn't hungry. His face had lost its color, and he spent sleepless nights, constantly fearing the inspector. If he had known the matter would escalate like this, he would never have done it. He had thought someone else would be suspected, and no one would think of him, but now it seemed like the truth would soon come out. The inspector's method of investigating made Jiyaram very uneasy.

On the seventh evening, Jiyaram returned home, deeply troubled. Until now, he had held onto some hope that he might escape, as the jewelry had not been found. But today, he had heard that the jewelry had been recovered. The inspector would be coming any moment with constables. There was no way out now. Perhaps bribing the inspector could suppress the case. He had money on hand, but how could this matter stay hidden? Even though the jewelry hadn't yet been recovered, the entire town was already gossiping that the son had stolen it. Once it was found, everyone would know, and he wouldn't be able to show his face anywhere.

Munshiji returned from the court that evening, visibly agitated. He held his head in his hands as he sat on the cot. Nirmala asked, "Why haven't you changed your clothes? You're later than usual today."

Munshiji replied, "Change clothes for what? Have you heard anything?"

Nirmala asked, "What happened? I haven't heard anything."

Munshiji said, "The jewelry has been found. Now it's impossible for Jiyaram to escape."

Nirmala wasn't surprised. Her face seemed to suggest that she already knew. She said, "I've been saying from the start, don't inform the police."

Munshiji asked, "You suspected Jiyaram?"

Nirmala replied, "Why wouldn't I? I saw him leaving my room."

Munshiji was stunned, "Then why didn't you tell me?"

Nirmala said, "This wasn't something for me to say. You would've thought I was accusing him out of spite. Tell me, wouldn't you have thought that? Don't lie."

Munshiji sighed, "It's possible, I won't deny it. But still, in that situation, you should've told me. We wouldn't have needed to file a report. You cared about your reputation, but didn't think of the consequences? I'm heading to the station now; Alayar Khan will be here soon!"

Nirmala asked, despairing, "And now?"

Munshiji looked up at the sky and said, "Now, whatever God wills. If I had one or two thousand rupees for a bribe, perhaps we could suppress the matter, but you know my situation. Fate is against us. I've sinned, and who will bear the punishment? One son was lost, and now this is happening to the other. He was a scoundrel, disrespectful, lazy—but he was still my son. He might have mended his ways eventually. This blow, I don't think I can bear."

Nirmala said, "If paying something can save him, I'll arrange the money."

Munshiji asked, "Can you? How much can you manage?"

Nirmala replied, "How much is needed?"

Munshiji said, "Probably not less than a thousand. I took a thousand from him in a case once. He'll make me pay that back today."

Nirmala said, "It will be done. Go to the station now."

It took Munshiji a long time at the station. It was a while before he got a chance to speak privately. Alayar Khan was a seasoned man—he didn't budge easily. Even after taking five hundred rupees, he acted as if he was doing a favor. But the job was done. On returning, Munshiji said to Nirmala, "Well, I managed to win the battle. You provided the money, but it was my words that did the work. It took a lot of effort, but he agreed. This won't be forgotten."

He then asked, "Has Jiyaram eaten?"

Nirmala replied, "No, he hasn't returned yet."

Munshiji said, "It must be nearly midnight."

Nirmala added, "I've gone to check several times, but his room is still dark."

Munshiji asked, "What about Siyaram?"

Nirmala replied, "He ate and went to sleep."

Munshiji asked, "Didn't you ask him where Jiyaram went?"

Nirmala said, "He said Jiyaram didn't tell him anything."

Munshiji felt suspicious. He woke Siyaram and asked, "Did Jiyaram tell you anything—when he'd be back, or where he was going?"

Siyaram rubbed his head and eyes and said, "He didn't say anything to me."

Munshiji asked, "Did he wear all his clothes when he left?"

Siyaram replied, "No, just his kurta and dhoti."

Munshiji asked, "Did he seem happy when he left?"

Siyaram said, "He didn't seem happy. He tried to come inside several times but turned back from the doorstep. He stood under the porch for several minutes. When he finally left, he was wiping his eyes. He's been crying often lately."

Munshiji sighed deeply, as if all meaning had left his life, and said to Nirmala, "You meant well, but no enemy could have struck me a harsher blow. If Jiyaram's mother were here, would she have hesitated like you did? Not at all."

Nirmala replied, "Why not go to Doctor Sinha's place? Maybe he's there. Many boys visit daily; perhaps one of them knows something. Despite all my caution, disgrace has still found its way to us."

Munshiji said, as if talking to an open window, "Yes, I'm going, what else can I do?"

As Munshiji stepped out, he saw Doctor Sinha standing there. Startled, he asked, "Have you been standing here long?"

Doctor Sinha replied, "No, I just arrived. Where are you going at this hour? It's half-past twelve."

Munshiji said, "I was coming to see you. Jiyaram hasn't returned yet. Has he come to your place?"

Doctor Sinha took both of Munshiji's hands in his and said, "Dear, now you must stay strong..." before Munshiji fell to the ground, like a man struck by a bullet.

## Chapter - 21

Rukmini looked at Nirmala, her expression hardened. "Will he go to school barefoot?" she asked.

Nirmala, braiding the hair of her young daughter, replied, "What can I do? I have no money."

Rukmini scoffed, "Money is saved for jewelry, but for the boy's shoes, there's never enough! Two have already left us, and now you want to drive the third one away as well?"

Nirmala sighed deeply, "Those who are meant to live will live, and those who are destined to die will die. I do not intend to kill or save anyone."

These days, Nirmala and Rukmini seemed to clash over something or the other every day. Since the jewelry was stolen, Nirmala's demeanor had changed drastically. She had become careful to the point of being miserly. Siyaram could cry his heart out, but he wouldn't get money for sweets. It wasn't just Siyaram facing this treatment; Nirmala herself would often postpone her own needs. Her sari would be worn until it was completely threadbare. For months, she wouldn't buy hair oil. Even milk for her little one became a rare indulgence. The thought of her infant's future loomed over her like a vast, dark cloud.

Munshiji had handed over all responsibilities to Nirmala. He did not interfere in her decisions, as if there was something within him that kept him subdued. He resumed attending court every day—something he hadn't done with such dedication even in his youth. His eyes were deteriorating, and Dr. Sinha had prohibited him from reading or writing at night. His digestion was already poor, and now he had developed asthma. Still, he would work tirelessly from dawn until midnight, irrespective of how his health was or how he felt. And Nirmala showed no pity towards him. It was the relentless anxiety about the future that had hardened her heart. She would grow angry at the mere sound of a beggar's voice—she could not bear the thought of spending even a single paisa.

One day, Nirmala sent Siyaram to buy ghee from the market. She no longer trusted Maid for these tasks. She didn't like Maid's ways, and Siyaram, though straightforward and honest, didn't know how to haggle. He ended up running errands for most of the household shopping. Nirmala weighed every item meticulously. If the weight of anything was even slightly off, she would send Siyaram back to return it. Much of his time was spent in this back-and-forth with the shopkeepers. Shopkeepers didn't readily sell goods to him—he was often turned away. Today was no different.

Siyaram brought back ghee after checking with several shops, convinced it was of good quality. But as soon as Nirmala sniffed it, she said, "This ghee is bad—take it back."

Frustrated, Siyaram retorted, "There is no better ghee in the entire market. I've checked several shops."

"So, I am lying?" Nirmala shot back.

"I'm not saying that," Siyaram replied. "But the shopkeeper clearly said he won't take it back. He told me to inspect it as much as I wanted before buying because once I bought it, he wouldn't return it. I smelled it, tasted it, and I bought it. Now, how can I return it?"

Nirmala ground her teeth. "The ghee is clearly mixed with tallow, and you're saying it's good? I won't use it in the kitchen. Do whatever you want—return it or eat it yourself."

Leaving the ghee pot there, Nirmala went inside. Siyaram felt a surge of anger and helplessness. How could he return it? The shopkeeper would outright refuse, and then what would he do? Several shopkeepers and people on the street would gather around, and he would be humiliated in front of them all. Shopkeepers already hesitated to sell anything to him. He wouldn't even be able to stand in front of a shop without being chastised. He thought to himself—let the ghee stay; I will not return it.

There is no one more unfortunate and dejected in this world than a motherless child. His mother came to his mind, and he thought, if she were here, would he have to endure all this? His brother was gone, and yet he was left alone to bear all these misfortunes. Tears welled up in his eyes, and he muttered to himself in a voice choked with emotion, "Mother, why have you forgotten me? Why won't you call me to you?"

Suddenly, Nirmala came back to the room. She had thought Siyaram had already left, but seeing him sitting there, she burst out in anger, "You're still sitting here? When will the food be cooked?"

Siyaram wiped his eyes and said, "I'll be late for school."

Nirmala snapped back, "If you're late for school one day, what's the harm? This is also work for the household, isn't it?"

"Every day it's the same thing," Siyaram retorted bitterly. "I'm never on time for school. I don't even get time to study at home. Every task you send me to do ends up being returned two or three times. I'm the one who gets scolded, the one who has to face embarrassment. It doesn't affect you."

"Yes, it doesn't affect me!" Nirmala shot back, her voice trembling. "I am your enemy, right? If it were my own son, I would care. But you? I only wish you never succeed, never get educated. I have nothing but evil in me, and you're innocent! A stepmother's name is tainted from the start. If one's own mother feeds poison, it becomes nectar; if I offer nectar, it becomes poison. I have given up everything for you people, spent my life crying, not even knowing why God made me. But to you, I am thriving at your expense. Yes, I find joy in tormenting you. Even God does not care to end my suffering."

Tears filled her eyes, and she stormed inside. Seeing her cry, Siyaram was stunned. He wasn't exactly repentant, but he feared what punishment might come. Quietly, he picked up the pot of ghee and headed to return it, much like a dog wandering into an unfamiliar village. Anyone who saw him could easily guess he was an orphan. As he got closer to the shop, his heart pounded with fear of the confrontation ahead. He made up his mind—if the shopkeeper refused to take back the ghee, he would leave it there and walk away. Surely the shopkeeper would then call him back.

He had even thought of the words he would use to argue with the shopkeeper: "Why, are you trying to deceive me? You showed one thing, but sold me another. Won't take it back, will you? Is this robbery?" But despite these resolutions, his steps were slow and hesitant. He didn't want the shopkeeper to see him coming from afar; he wanted to appear suddenly in front of him. And so, he took a roundabout way through another alley to the shop.

The shopkeeper, seeing him approach, said, "I already told you, I don't take back items. Didn't I say that?"

Siyaram, frustrated, said, "You didn't give me the ghee you showed! You showed me one thing, then sold me another. Why won't you take it back? What sort of trickery is this?"

The shopkeeper replied, "If there's better ghee in the market, then I will pay the penalty. Take the pot and check at a few other shops."

Siyaram retorted, "I don't have the time for this. Take back your ghee."

"I will not take it back," the shopkeeper said adamantly.

A dreadlocked sadhu, sitting nearby, had been watching the entire scene. He approached Siyaram, took a sniff of the ghee, and said, "Child, this ghee seems very good."

The shopkeeper, now emboldened, added, "Sir, we don't sell subpar goods to our customers. Only unknowing customers might receive poor-quality goods."

The sadhu, looking at Siyaram with compassionate eyes, as if eager to help, said, "Take it, child. The ghee is good."

Siyaram started crying. He no longer had any proof to discredit the ghee. He said, sobbing, "She says the ghee isn't good and wants me to return it. I told her it was fine."

The sadhu asked, "Who says so?"

"Must be his mother," the shopkeeper interjected. "No goods seem to please her. She makes the poor boy run around endlessly. She's his stepmother, after all. If it were his real mother, she would have thought twice before doing this."

The sadhu looked at Siyaram with sympathy, his heart aching for the boy. He said in a gentle voice, "How long has it been since your mother passed, child?"

"It's been six years," Siyaram replied.

"You must have been very young then," the sadhu said softly. "Oh, Lord, how mysterious are Your ways! You've taken away this little boy's mother's love. Such a tragedy. Six years old, and to be at the mercy of a wicked stepmother! Oh, Lord, You are truly merciless! Shopkeeper, have pity on the boy—take the ghee back. Otherwise, his mother will not let him stay in the house. By God's grace, your ghee will be sold soon. My blessings are with you."

The shopkeeper did not return the money. Eventually, the boy had no choice but to return to get the ghee again. Who knows how many times he'd have to go back during the day and whom he might encounter among the schemers along the way? The best quality ghee in shop was given to Siyaram. Siyaram genuinely believed the sadhu's intervention had resulted in him getting the best quality.

Carrying the ghee, the sadhu walked with Siyaram. Along the way, they talked. "Child, my mother, too, left me when I was just three years old. Whenever I see motherless children, my heart aches," the sadhu said.

Siyaram asked, "Did your father also remarry?"

"Yes," the sadhu replied. "Otherwise, why would I have become a sadhu? At first, my father refused to remarry and loved me dearly, but then something changed. He remarried, and my stepmother, as beautiful as she was, was equally harsh. She wouldn't give me food all day, and if I cried, she would beat me. My father's heart turned against me too. He grew to despise me, and if he heard me cry, he would beat me. Eventually, I left home."

Siyaram had often thought of running away himself, and the thought arose once more. He asked eagerly, "Where did you go after leaving home?"

The sadhu smiled and said, "The day I was freed from the bondage of home was the day all my sufferings ended. The day fear left my heart, it felt as though I was liberated. I sat under a bridge all day. In the evening, I met a great sage—Swami Amritanandji. He was a lifelong celibate and took pity on me. He took me in, and I traveled far and wide with him. He was a great yogi, and he taught me the secrets of yoga. I practiced so much that now I can see my mother whenever I wish and even talk to her."

Siyaram's eyes widened in amazement. "But your mother passed away, didn't she?"

The sadhu nodded. "Yes, child, but through yoga, one can summon any departed soul."

"If I learn yoga, will I be able to see my mother too?" Siyaram asked eagerly.

The sadhu smiled, "Of course, with practice, anything is possible. But you need a worthy guru. Yoga can help you achieve great powers—summon as much wealth as you want in an instant, heal any illness."

"Where is your ashram?" Siyaram asked.

"Child, I don't have a fixed place. I wander from one region to another. But for now, go to school. I must also go for my prayers."

Siyaram pleaded, "Please, let me accompany you. I haven't had enough of your company."

"No, child. You are already late for school," the sadhu said.

"When will I see you again?" Siyaram asked.

"I will come again someday, child. Where is your home?"

Siyaram, now cheerful, said, "Will you come to my home? It's very close. It would be such an honor."

Siyaram walked ahead, guiding the sadhu, his heart filled with joy, as if he was carrying a treasure. Reaching the house, he said, "Please, sit for a while."

"No, child. Not today. Perhaps tomorrow or the day after. Is this your home?"

"Yes. When will you come tomorrow?" Siyaram asked eagerly.

"I cannot say for sure. But I will come sometime," the sadhu replied.

The sadhu continued walking, and a short distance away, he met another sadhu named Hariharanand. Parmanand asked, "Where have you been wandering? Any luck with a new recruit?"

Hariharanand sighed, "I've been roaming everywhere, but no luck. And those I found made fun of me."

Parmanand smiled slyly, "I think I've found one. Let's see if he gets caught in the trap."

Hariharanand shook his head. "You always say that, but they leave after a day or two."

Parmanand replied confidently, "Not this time. Just wait and see. His mother is dead. His father remarried, and the stepmother is cruel. The boy is fed up with his home."

"Excellent," Hariharanand nodded approvingly. "That's the best way. We should first find out which homes have stepmothers and then lay the trap there."

## Chapter - 22

Nirmala scolded, "What took you so long?"

Siyaram replied with defiance, "I fell asleep somewhere on the way."

"I'm not saying that," Nirmala retorted, "but do you even know what time it is? It's already past ten. The market isn't even that far."

"Not far at all," Siyaram muttered, "It's right at the doorstep."

"Why don't you speak properly? You're acting like you're doing me a favor by running my errands!"

Siyaram snapped back, "Then why do you keep complaining? Returning goods is not easy. I had to argue with the shopkeeper for hours. It was only because of a Sadhu's intervention that he agreed. Otherwise, he wouldn't have taken it back at all. I didn't stop anywhere for a moment; I came straight home."

Nirmala fumed, "You went out to get ghee and returned at eleven. If you go out for firewood, you'll be back by dusk. Your father left without eating because of you. If you were going to take this long, why didn't you just say so earlier? You could have gone for the firewood first."

Siyaram could no longer hold himself back. He shouted, "Send someone else for the firewood! I'm already late for school."

"Aren't you going to eat?" Nirmala asked.

"No, I won't," Siyaram retorted.

"I'm ready to cook. But I can't go fetch firewood," Nirmala responded.

"Then why not send Maid?" Siyaram suggested.

"Have you ever seen the quality of what Maid brings?" Nirmala replied, shaking her head.

"Well, I'm not going right now," Siyaram insisted.

"Don't blame me then," Nirmala said sharply.

Siyaram had not been to school in days. The endless household errands left him with no time to study. What awaited him at school anyway? Scolding from the teachers, standing in the corner, or being made to wear the tall dunce hat. He would leave home with his books, only to go sit under a tree outside the city or watch the soldiers' drill. At three o'clock, he would return home. Today was no different—he left the house but couldn't concentrate. His stomach grumbled in hunger. How sad, he thought, that he had to go without food today. It wasn't impossible to prepare food by ten, was it? He understood that Father had left without eating, but was there really not even a few coins left for him? If Mother had been here, she would never have let him leave like this, without anything to eat or drink. He had no one now.

A longing for Sadhu Ji's presence overwhelmed Siyaram. Where would he be at this hour? Where should he go to find him? He longed to hear Sadhu Parmanand's comforting words and feel his encouragement. He thought, why didn't I just go with him in the first place? What was left for me here at home? He decided not to return home but went straight to the ghee shop, hoping to find Sadhu Ji there. But Sadhu Ji wasn't there. After standing around for a long time, Siyaram returned home. He had just sat down when Nirmala approached him.

"What took you so long today? No breakfast was made in the morning, and now again, you're going without food. Go to the market and get some vegetables."

Siyaram, now frustrated, said, "I've come back starving, and you haven't even brought me a drop of water to drink, and now you're ordering me to go to the market. I'm not going. I'm nobody's servant. All you give me is dry bread. If that's what it takes, I'll earn it through my own labor. If I must work, I won't do it for you. Don't bother cooking anything for me."

Nirmala stood there, stunned. What had gotten into the boy today? Usually, he would quietly do as he was told. Why was he acting up today? Even now, it didn't occur to her to give Siyaram a few coins for something to eat. Her nature had become so miserly. She said coldly,

"Helping out at home isn't considered labor. If I said I wouldn't cook, or if your father decided not to go to court, what would happen then? Tell me. If you don't want to go, don't go. I'll send Maid instead. How was I to know that you dislike going to the market? Otherwise, I would never have sent you, even if it meant paying double. Alright then, I swear I won't send you again."

Siyaram felt a twinge of guilt but still refused to go to the market. His thoughts were occupied with Sadhu Ji. All his miseries and hopes for the future seemed now tied to Sadhu Ji's blessings. He felt that by surrendering himself to Sadhu Ji, his otherwise aimless life would find purpose. By sunset, he grew restless. He scoured the entire market but found no trace of Sadhu Parmanand. Hungry and thirsty from dawn to dusk, the young boy wandered the streets, lanes, and temples, searching for that sanctuary without which his life had grown unbearable. At one point, he spotted a sadhu standing in front of a temple. He thought it was Sadhu Parmanand Ji and ran up, only to realize it was another ascetic. Crestfallen, he moved on.

Gradually, the streets grew deserted, doors of houses closed, and people began laying out mats and sacks on the pavements for their night's sleep. But Siyaram did not return home. His heart had grown cold toward that house where no one loved him, where he lived like an outsider simply because he had nowhere else to go. Who would even care that he hadn't returned home yet? Father would be resting after his meal, and Nirmala would be retiring for the night. Would anyone have even peeked into his room to check on him? Yes, Aunt Rukmini might be worried; she would still be waiting for him. She wouldn't eat until he returned.

The thought of Rukmini made Siyaram turn back home. If nothing else, she would at least hold him close and cry. She would keep some water ready for him to wash his hands and face when he returned. Not all children in this world sip milk or eat gold-plated morsels. Many don't even get a full meal, but only those deprived of motherly love become estranged from their homes. As Siyaram began walking towards home, he suddenly saw Sadhu Paramanand coming down an alley.

Siyaram rushed over and grabbed his hand. Startled, Paramanand asked, "Child, what are you doing here?"

Siyaram quickly made up an excuse, "I came to see a friend. How far is your ashram from here?"

"We are leaving here today," Paramanand said. "We are heading to Haridwar."

Disheartened, Siyaram asked, "Are you leaving today itself?"

"Yes, child, but I will come back, and when I do, I will visit you."

In a trembling voice, Siyaram said, "I want to come with you."

"With me?" Paramanand asked, surprised. "Will your family let you come?"

"My family doesn't care about me," Siyaram replied.

Beyond that, Siyaram could say no more. His tear-filled eyes told a tale of sorrow far greater than any words could express. Paramanand pulled the boy into an embrace and said, "Alright, child, if you wish to come, then come. Enjoy the company of saints and sages. If it is God's will, your desire will be fulfilled."

*The bird circling above the grain finally fell to it. What would be the fate of his life—whether it ended in a cage or beneath a hunter's knife—who could say?*

## Chapter - 23

Munshiji returned from the court at five in the evening and collapsed onto the cot. His aging body, compounded by an entire day without food, was visibly weary. His mouth was parched, and Nirmala could instantly tell that the day had been unproductive. She asked gently, "Didn't get anything today?"

Munshiji replied, "The whole day was spent running around, but nothing came of it."

"What happened in the criminal case?" Nirmala asked.

"My client was convicted," he said, shaking his head.

"And what about the case with the Pandit?" she probed further.

"The judgment went against him," Munshiji replied.

"But you were confident that the claim would be dismissed," Nirmala reminded him.

Munshiji sighed deeply. "I was confident, yes. But who has the time to work things out thoroughly these days?"

"And the civil case?" Nirmala asked cautiously.

"We lost that too," Munshiji said flatly.

"So, today you must have encountered someone really unlucky in the morning," Nirmala quipped bitterly.

Munshiji had reached a stage where work had almost entirely dried up. The few cases that did come to him rarely ended in his favor. Yet, he tried his best to conceal his failures from Nirmala. On days when he earned nothing, he would borrow a few rupees from friends to hand over to her, but now even that avenue was exhausted.

In a tone full of concern, Nirmala remarked, "With income like this, only God can sustain us. On top of that, Siyaram barely go to market to purchase goods. Even simple tasks are left to the maid. He came back with the ghee at eleven, and no matter how much I begged, he refused to buy firewood."

Munshiji, looking tired, asked, “So you didn’t cook anything?”

“How could I cook without firewood?” Nirmala replied sharply. “It’s these little things that cause you to lose cases. Can anyone cook without fuel?”

Munshiji said, almost to himself, “So he left without eating anything?”

Nirmala sighed. “What was there at home to feed him? I had nothing to give.”

Gathering courage, Munshiji asked, “You didn’t give him any money?”

Nirmala scowled and snapped, “Do you think money grows on trees in this house?”

Munshiji fell silent. He waited, hoping Nirmala might offer him something to eat, but when even a glass of water didn’t arrive, he left dejectedly. Reflecting on Siyaram’s hardship, Munshiji’s heart grew restless. Couldn’t Maid have been sent to fetch the firewood? Would it have been such a loss? What’s the use of such extreme thrift when the family ends up hungry?

Desperate, Munshiji rummaged through his small wooden box, hoping to find a few coins. He emptied all the papers from it, inspecting each one carefully, but there was nothing. Then, as fate would have it, while shaking out the papers, a single coin fell out. Overjoyed, Munshiji felt a flicker of hope. He had earned much larger sums in the past, but the joy this small coin brought him in that moment was unparalleled.

He held the coin tightly and went to Siyaram’s room, calling for him. There was no response. Entering the room, he found it empty. Siyaram was nowhere to be seen. Was he still at school? The question weighed heavily on Munshiji’s mind. He went inside and asked Maid, who confirmed that Siyaram had already returned from school.

“Did he have anything to eat?” Munshiji inquired further.

Maid, without turning, wrinkled her nose and walked away silently.

Munshiji slowly returned to his room. For the first time, he felt anger toward Nirmala, but the moment passed, and the anger turned inward. Lying on the bare floor in the darkened room, he cursed himself for being so indifferent toward his son. Exhausted from the day's trials, he eventually fell asleep.

Later, Maid called out, "Sir, dinner is ready." Munshiji woke with a start. The lamp in the room was lit.

"What time is it? I must've fallen asleep," he asked groggily.

"Its Nine o'clock" Maid replied.

"Has Siyaram come back?" Munshiji asked.

"If he's come back, he must be at home," Maid said dismissively.

Annoyed, Munshiji snapped, "I'm asking if he's back. Why do you keep rambling? Has he come or not?"

"I haven't seen him. Why should I lie?" Maid replied bluntly.

Munshiji lay down again, muttering, "Let him return first; then I'll come to eat."

For the next half-hour, he lay staring toward the door, waiting. Finally, he got up and went outside. Walking two furlongs to the right, he turned back and returned to the house, calling out, "Has Siyaram come?"

A voice from inside replied, "Not yet."

He walked to the left, going as far as the alley's corner, but there was still no sign of Siyaram. Returning home, he asked again, "Has Siyaram come?"

The reply remained the same: "No."

As the clock struck ten, Munshiji hurried toward the Company Garden, thinking perhaps Siyaram had gone there and fallen asleep on the grass. Reaching the garden, he searched every bench, wandered in every direction, and called out Siyaram's name loudly, but there was no response. He thought of the school and began walking in that direction but stopped halfway. The market was closed, and it was far too late for any school event.

Still clinging to hope, Munshiji returned home. He stood by the door and called out, “Has Siyaram come?” The door was shut, and no one answered. He called again, louder this time. Maid opened the door and said, “He hasn’t come yet.”

Munshiji called her over and asked in a pained voice, “You know everything that happens in this house. Tell me, what happened today?”

The maid hesitated but finally replied, “Sir, why should I lie? Mistress will dismiss me, but it’s true—nobody treats another’s child like their own. He’s sent to the market constantly. Today, when he refused to fetch firewood, the stove wasn’t even lit. And if you don’t see these things, who else will?”

“Tell her I’m not eating tonight,” Munshiji replied flatly and went back to his room.

He sat down heavily, sighing deeply. With a trembling voice, he muttered, “Oh, God, haven’t I suffered enough? Are you going to take even this final support from me?”

Nirmala entered the room and said, “Siyaram hasn’t returned yet. I kept telling him I’d prepare dinner if he wanted to eat, but who knows when he left. I don’t know where he’s wandering. He doesn’t listen to anything I say. How long should I keep waiting for him? You should eat now. I’ll set aside food for him.”

Munshiji looked at her with stern eyes and asked, “What time is it now?”

“I don’t know. Maybe ten?” Nirmala replied, unsure.

“No, it’s already midnight,” Munshiji said grimly.

“Midnight? He’s never stayed out this late before,” Nirmala remarked. “How long will you keep waiting for him? He didn’t even eat lunch today. I’ve never seen such a restless boy.”

"Why does it bother you so much?" Munshiji asked irritably.

"Just look at the time! It's so late, and there's no sign of him," she said with exasperation.

"Perhaps this is his last mischief," Munshiji muttered quietly.

"What are you saying? Where will he go? He's probably staying with some friend," Nirmala said, trying to reassure him.

"Maybe. Let's hope that's the case. May God make it so," Munshiji replied with a heavy heart.

"If he comes back in the morning, make sure to scold him," Nirmala said firmly.

"Oh, I'll do much more than that," Munshiji said with resolve.

"Please eat now. It's been so long," Nirmala pleaded.

"I'll eat after scolding him in the morning. If he doesn't return, where will you find such a dutiful servant?" Munshiji remarked bitterly.

Annoyed, Nirmala retorted, "So, are you saying I drove him away?"

"No, who's saying that? Why would you drive him away? He used to do your work, but maybe he just had bad luck," Munshiji replied.

Nirmala didn't say anything further. Fearing the argument might escalate, she went inside without even asking him to sleep. A short while later, Maid closed the inner doors.

How could Munshiji possibly sleep? Out of three sons, only one was left, and now even he seemed to be slipping away. What was left in life but darkness? There would be no one to even carry his name forward. Alas, how many gems had slipped through his fingers? Tears streamed down Munshiji's face; it was no surprise. In the overwhelming sorrow and suffocating guilt, a faint glimmer of hope still kept him afloat. But what would happen when even that glimmer faded? Who could imagine his agony?

Several times, Munshiji's eyes closed briefly, but each time he startled awake, mistaking any sound for Siyaram's return.

At dawn, he went out again to search for his son. He felt ashamed to ask anyone about Siyaram. What would he say? Who would sympathize? Without saying it openly, everyone would think, You reap what you sow.

The entire day, Munshiji wandered through school grounds, markets, and gardens. Despite going two days without food, he mustered a strength only he could explain. By midnight, Munshiji returned home. A lantern was lit at the door, and Nirmala stood waiting.

As soon as she saw him, she said, “You didn’t even tell me you were going out. Who knows when you left. Did you find any trace of him?”

Munshiji, with fiery eyes, snapped, “Get out of my way, or you’ll regret it. I’m not in my senses. This is all because of you. You’re the reason for my condition today. Six years ago, this house wasn’t like this. You’ve destroyed everything I built. You ruined the flourishing garden I had. Only one withered tree remains, and you won’t rest until you’ve uprooted that too. I didn’t bring you into this house to destroy me. I wanted to make my life happier. This is my penance.”

He paused, then continued with despair, “Those boys, who once were like jewels in my life, have been turned into servants in my own home because of you. And I stood by, blind, watching it all happen. Go ahead, fetch me some poison. Let’s complete this destruction.”

Tears welled up in Nirmala’s eyes. “I am cursed,” she said. Who knows why God gave me life? But how can you be so certain Siyaram won’t return?”

As Munshiji walked toward his room, he muttered, “Don’t provoke me. Go ahead and celebrate. Your wish has been fulfilled.”

Nirmala cried all night. Such disgrace! Even after witnessing Jiyaram stealing the jewelry, she had not dared to speak out. Why? Because people would accuse her of fabricating lies to harm her stepson. Now her silence was being used against her. If she had confronted Jiyaram at that moment and he had run away in shame, wouldn’t the blame still have fallen on her?

What wrong had she ever done to Siyaram? She had only sent him to run errands to save money. Was she saving for herself? Did she plan to buy jewelry for her own use? With their current income, every penny counted. What other means did she have to save for the family? Life was so uncertain; she couldn't rely on anyone—young or old. For her daughter's wedding, who would she turn to for help? The responsibility wasn't hers alone. She was only trying to secure the future for her husband and son. Who else would bear the burden of arranging for the girl's wedding?

Yet, despite all her sacrifices, disgrace was her only reward.

By noon, the stove still hadn't been lit. Eating was essential for life, yet no one seemed to care. Munshiji lay lifeless outside while Nirmala sat inside. Their daughter wandered in and out, hoping someone would speak to her. She often stood by Siyaram's door, calling, "Brother, Brother," but no one responded.

In the evening, Munshiji returned and asked Nirmala, "Do you have any money?"

Startled, she asked, "What do you need it for?"

"Just answer my question," Munshiji demanded.

"Don't you already know? You're the one who gives me money," she retorted.

"I'm asking if you have any or not. If you do, give it to me. If not, just say so," he said impatiently.

Nirmala hesitated and replied evasively, "If there is any, it must be in the house. I haven't sent it anywhere else."

Munshiji walked away, knowing full well that Nirmala had money but didn't want to give it. Her response confirmed his suspicions.

At nine o'clock that night, Munshiji went to Rukmini and said, "Sister, I'm going out for a bit. Ask Maid to pack my bedding and place a few clothes in the trunk."

Rukmini, who was cooking, asked, "Why don't you ask Nirmala directly? Where are you planning to go?"

"I'm telling you, not her. Would I have asked you if I wanted to tell her? Why are you cooking tonight?" Munshiji asked.

"Who else will cook? Nirmala says she has a headache. But why leave now? Can't it wait until morning?" Rukmini said.

"I've been delaying it for three days already. I'll search around—maybe I'll find a lead about Siyaram. Some people say they saw him talking to a Sadhu. Maybe he's been misled," Munshiji replied.

"How long will you be gone?" Rukmini asked.

"I don't know—maybe a week, maybe a month. Who can say?" Munshiji replied wearily.

Munshiji sat down to eat. Observing his weariness and despair, Nirmala felt a wave of compassion for him. Her anger melted away, leaving only concern. She didn't say anything directly but gently woke their daughter, coaxing her, "Go ask your father where he's going."

The little girl peeked out from behind the door and asked, "Father, where are you going?"

Munshiji, his voice softening at the sight of his daughter, replied, "I'm going far away, dear, to look for your brother."

Standing where she was, the child asked, "Can I come too?"

Munshiji smiled faintly and said, "It's very far, child. I'll bring back toys for you. Come here; why don't you?"

The little girl giggled and hid herself but peeked out again moments later, asking, "Why won't you take me with you?"

Munshiji, pretending to chide her gently, replied, "Because you never come to me when I call."

The girl, now emboldened, toddled over and climbed into his lap. For a few fleeting moments, Munshiji forgot his sorrow, immersed in her innocent prattle. Her small hands, her laughter, and her sparkling eyes momentarily eased the weight in his heart. He played with her, his grief momentarily buried under her cheerful banter.

After finishing his meal, Munshiji stood to leave. Nirmala watched him from the window, silently debating whether she should stop him. Her heart urged her to hand him some money, but her hesitation restrained her. Finally, unable to hold back, she approached Rukmini and pleaded, “Sister, please talk to him. Find out where he’s going. My words won’t reach him, but yours might. It seems pointless—where will he even search?”

Rukmini looked at her with compassionate eyes but said nothing. She quietly withdrew into her room.

Nirmala sat with her daughter in her lap, lost in thought. Perhaps he would come to see the child before leaving or even come to speak to her. But her hopes were in vain. Munshiji picked up his bedding and trunk and stepped outside. He climbed into the waiting tonga without a word.

At that moment, a crushing sense of finality gripped Nirmala. Her heart ached, and she felt as though this departure would mark the end. Desperate, she rushed to the door, ready to call him back, but the tonga had already pulled away.

## Chapter - 24

Days passed by. A month slipped away, but there was no word from Munshiji. He hadn't returned, nor had he sent any letter. Nirmala was consumed by a singular fear—what if he never came back? Her worries weren't about what he might be going through, where he might be wandering, or how his health might be. Her anxiety revolved entirely around her own survival and, even more so, that of her child. How would she manage the household? How would God help her through this ordeal? What would become of her daughter?

The small savings she had carefully managed through stringent thrift were diminishing day by day. Each time she took even a single coin from it, it felt as if her blood was being drained. In frustration, she cursed Munshiji. If her daughter cried for something, Nirmala's frustration often boiled over, and she lashed out, calling the child unlucky and cursed. Her once kind and nurturing demeanor had grown harsh. Even Rukmini's presence in the house now felt like an unbearable burden, as though she were an added weight on her shoulders. When a heart is heavy with anguish, the words it utters burn like fire.

Nirmala, once known for her gentle and sweet nature, had transformed into someone sharp-tongued and irritable. Her words were no longer soft or kind, and the sweetness that once characterized her personality had vanished. Even Maid, who had served the household for many years and was patient by nature, could no longer endure Nirmala's constant scolding and eventually left. Nirmala's affection for her daughter, whom she once loved more than life itself, had also soured. The child's presence now annoyed her, and she scolded and sometimes even struck her over trivial matters. The little girl, with nowhere else to turn, found solace in Rukmini's arms. Rukmini would comfort and console her, holding her close as the child wept. For the little girl, Rukmini had become the only refuge.

Amid this turmoil, the only thing that seemed to bring Nirmala any relief was her time spent with Sudha. She often looked for excuses to visit her friend, relishing those moments of escape. However, she had stopped taking her daughter along. Earlier, when the child could eat and play freely at Sudha's home, she had enjoyed herself. But now, the child's hunger often surfaced during these visits, and she would beg for food, much to Nirmala's embarrassment. Nirmala would glare at her threateningly, clenching her fists, but the child's cries of hunger would not stop. To avoid such situations, Nirmala began leaving her daughter behind.

When at Sudha's home, Nirmala felt like a different person. Sitting with her friend, she could momentarily forget her worries, much like a drunkard who loses himself in the haze of intoxication. At Sudha's house, Nirmala felt like a human again. Those moments freed her from the weight of her anxieties. Her demeanor changed entirely; the harsh, irritable woman at home transformed into a figure of warmth and humor. The same Nirmala who was sharp-tongued and bitter at home became jovial and sweet at Sudha's place. It was as if her suppressed youthful nature found an outlet there. She would dress neatly, styling her hair and wearing her best clothes, leaving her sorrows at the door. She went there to laugh, not to cry.

*But perhaps this small respite was not meant to last.*

Nirmala usually visited Sudha in the afternoons or late evenings. However, one day, feeling particularly restless, she went early in the morning. Sudha had gone to the river for a bath, and Dr. Sinha was getting ready to leave for the hospital. The maid was busy with her chores. Nirmala, unaware of Sudha's absence, settled into her friend's room, assuming Sudha would return shortly. After waiting for a few minutes, she picked up a book of pictures from the shelf and, loosening her hair, lay down on the bed to browse through it.

Meanwhile, Dr. Sinha, searching for his glasses, entered the room. He walked in without hesitation, not realizing anyone was there. Seeing

Nirmala lying on the bed with her hair undone, he froze. Startled, Nirmala sat up abruptly, quickly covering her head with her dupatta and standing up. Embarrassed, Dr. Sinha mumbled, "I'm sorry, Nirmala. I didn't know you were here. I was just looking for my glasses. I thought it might be here."

Nirmala, spotting the glasses case on the shelf, retrieved it and handed it to him, her eyes lowered and her body tense with discomfort. As she extended the case toward him, Dr. Sinha reached out, his hands trembling. Though he took the glasses, he didn't leave. He stood there, seemingly lost.

Feeling uneasy, Nirmala asked, "Has Sudha gone somewhere?"

"Yes, she went for a bath," Dr. Sinha replied without meeting her gaze. Yet, he remained rooted in place.

"When will she return?" Nirmala asked again, her unease growing.

"She should be back soon," he said, still not moving.

Fearing the awkwardness of the moment, Nirmala said, "Perhaps she's taking her time. I should leave now."

At this, Dr. Sinha finally raised his head. His voice trembled with an emotion he could no longer suppress. "No, Nirmala, she'll be back soon. Stay a while. Every day you visit for Sudha's sake. Today, stay for mine. How long must I burn in this fire alone? I speak the truth, Nirmala..."

Nirmala heard no more. It felt as though the earth beneath her feet was spinning, as though her soul had been struck by a thousand thunderbolts. Grabbing a shawl from the clothesline, she fled the room without a word. Dr. Sinha, stunned and humiliated, stood there, unable to stop her or say anything further.

As Nirmala reached the door, she saw Sudha stepping out of a tonga. Without giving her a chance to speak, Nirmala brushed past her like an arrow, leaving Sudha bewildered.

Sudha stood there, confused and concerned. She hurried inside to ask the maid what had happened. She would find out the culprit and if she came to know that the maid or any other servant had said something insulting to her, she would fire her on the spot. Entering her room, she found Dr. Sinha sitting on the bed, looking pale and dejected.

“Did Nirmala come here?” she asked, her tone sharp.

“Yes, she did,” Dr. Sinha replied hesitantly, scratching his head.

“Did the maid say something to her? She left without saying a word to me. She looked upset,” Sudha pressed.

Dr. Sinha’s face grew paler. “No one said anything to her,” he replied weakly.

Sudha wasn’t convinced. “I’ll find out. If anyone insulted her, I swear they’ll be gone by the end of the day.”

Flustered, Dr. Sinha stammered, “I didn’t hear anyone say anything to her. Maybe she didn’t see you.”

“She didn’t see me? That’s absurd! I stepped out of the tonga right in front of her. She even glanced at me but didn’t say a word. Did she come into this room?” Sudha asked pointedly.

Dr. Sinha’s heart pounded. Hesitating, he admitted, “Yes, she did.”

“Then what happened? Did you say something to her?” Sudha’s suspicions sharpened.

“No! Why would I say anything? Do you think I’m foolish?” he said defensively.

“Then why didn’t you leave when you saw her here?” Sudha demanded.

Dr. Sinha, now desperate, said, “I wasn’t even in the room. I was outside looking for my glasses. When I didn’t find it there, I thought it might be inside. When I entered, I saw her sitting here. I was about to leave when she asked me what I was looking for. I told her about the glasses, and she handed them to me. That’s all.”

"Just that, and she stormed out? Why?" Sudha pressed further.

Dr. Sinha protested weakly, "She didn't storm out angrily. She was about to leave, and I simply said, 'Wait, Sudha will be back soon.' When she didn't stay, what could I do?"

Sudha frowned, her mind racing. "Something about this doesn't make sense. I'll go see her and find out what's wrong."

Dr. Sinha grew uneasy. "Do you really need to go right now? There's plenty of time later."

Wrapping a shawl around herself, Sudha replied firmly, "I can't wait. My stomach is churning with worry, and you're telling me to delay?"

Without waiting for another word, Sudha strode briskly toward Nirmala's home. In less than five minutes, she arrived at Nirmala's house."

Nirmala lay on her cot in her room, sobbing, while her little daughter stood beside her, asking, "Mother, why are you crying?" Sudha picked up the child in her arms and asked Nirmala, "Sister, tell me the truth, what happened? Did someone say something to you at my house? I've asked everyone, but no one is telling me anything."

Wiping her tears, Nirmala replied, "No one said anything, sister. Who would say anything to me there?"

Sudha pressed further, "Then why didn't you speak to me and started crying as soon as you came back?"

Nirmala sighed deeply and said, "I'm crying over my fate, what else?"

Sudha, refusing to let it go, said, "If you don't tell me, I will make you swear."

Nirmala pleaded, "Don't make me swear, sister. No one said anything to me. Who would I blame falsely?"

Sudha wasn't convinced. "Swear on me," she insisted.

Nirmala looked defeated. "You're being unreasonable," she said.

Sudha, her voice tinged with hurt, retorted, "If you don't tell me, Nirmala, I'll think you don't care for me at all. It's all just empty words. I don't hide anything from you, but you treat me as a stranger. I had so much faith in you. Now I know no one can truly be trusted."

Sudha's eyes filled with tears. She put the child down and turned to leave.

Nirmala, overcome with emotion, quickly got up, grabbed Sudha's hand, and, crying, said, "Sudha, I beg you, please don't ask me. It will only bring you pain, and I may never be able to show you my face again. If I weren't so cursed, would I have to see such days? Now, all I pray for is that God takes me away from this world. If things are so terrible now, I can't even imagine what worse might lie ahead."

The meaning behind these words did not escape the perceptive Sudha. She immediately understood that Dr. Sinha had done something inappropriate. His hesitation while speaking, his attempts to avoid her questions, and his guilty, pale expression came rushing back to her mind. From head to toe, she trembled with rage, and without saying another word, she stormed toward the door, furious like a lioness.

Nirmala tried to stop her, but she couldn't. Within moments, Sudha was out on the street, heading straight toward her home. Nirmala collapsed to the ground and broke into uncontrollable sobs.

## Chapter - 25

Nirmala lay on her cot the entire day. It seemed as though life had drained out of her body. She neither bathed nor got up to eat. By evening, she developed a fever. Her body burned like a furnace throughout the night. The next day, the fever didn't subside, though it did lessen slightly. She lay motionless on the cot, her vacant eyes fixed on the door. Everything felt empty—inside and out. No worries, no memories, no pain. Even the power of thought seemed to have abandoned her.

Suddenly, Rukmini appeared, holding the child in her arms.

Nirmala asked, "Was she crying a lot?"

Rukmini replied, "No, not even a sob. She lay quietly the whole night. Sudha sent a little milk."

Nirmala asked hesitantly, "Didn't the milkmaid come?"

Rukmini replied, "She said to give her the overdue payment first, then she'd bring it. How are you feeling now?"

Nirmala sighed, "There's nothing wrong with me. I just had a fever yesterday."

Rukmini said, "Dr. Sinha is in a terrible state."

Startled, Nirmala asked, "What happened? Is he alright?"

Rukmini replied, "Alright? Preparations are being made to carry his dead body! Some say he consumed poison, others say his heart simply stopped. Only God knows what happened."

Nirmala drew a deep, heavy breath. Her voice choked as she said, "Oh God! What will happen to Sudha? How will she survive?" She burst into tears and sobbed for a long time.

Then, with great difficulty, she prepared herself to visit Sudha. Her legs trembled, and she had to hold onto the wall for support, but her heart wouldn't let her stay. She was tormented by thoughts of what Sudha might have said to her husband after leaving here. "I didn't even say anything to her. Who knows what meaning she drew from my words? Oh, such a kind, noble soul—what a tragic end!"

If Nirmala had known that her outburst would lead to such a horrifying outcome, she would have swallowed her anger and laughed it off. The realization that her harshness had caused Dr. Sinha's demise tore her heart to shreds. She felt a pain so intense, it was as though her heart was being pierced by thorns.

She reached Dr. Sinha's house. The body had already been taken away. An eerie silence hung outside. Inside, the house was filled with women. Sudha sat on the floor, weeping uncontrollably. Seeing Nirmala, she cried even louder and clung to her chest. The two of them wept together for a long time.

When the crowd of women thinned, and they were alone, Nirmala asked gently, "What happened, sister? What did you say to him?"

Sudha had already grappled with this question in her mind countless times. The answer that had brought her some semblance of peace was the one she now gave to Nirmala.

"I couldn't stay silent, sister," Sudha replied. "Such things only make one angry. What could I do?"

Nirmala protested, "But I didn't even say anything to you that could cause such a reaction."

Sudha sighed, "You couldn't have, Nirmala. But he told me what happened. And I... I said whatever came to my tongue. When an idea takes root in the heart, you have to assume it's done. Given the right moment and opportunity, it's bound to manifest. It's no use saying, 'I was just joking.' Words spoken in private reveal intent.

"I never told you this, but I had caught him glancing at you several times. Back then, I thought maybe I was imagining things. Now I know what those glances meant! If I had more experience of the world, I would never have let you come to my house. At the very least, I would have ensured you never crossed his path. But how was I to know that men's mouths speak one thing while their hearts harbor another?

"What happened was God's will. Still, I consider myself fortunate to be widowed. A poor person is far happier than a wealthy one whose wealth turns into a venomous snake that strikes at him. It's easier to fast than to consume poisoned food."

Just then, Dr. Sinha's younger brother and Krishna entered the house. The wailing inside grew louder.

# Chapter - 26

Another month passed. On the third day after her husband's passing, Sudha left with her brother-in-law. Now, Nirmala was utterly alone. Earlier, she would find solace in talking and laughing, but now, her only recourse was tears. Her health deteriorated further day by day. The rent for their old house was too high, so she moved to a smaller, cheaper house. It was in a narrow alley with a single room and a small courtyard. Neither light nor fresh air entered the place; the stench was unbearable.

Her meals became irregular. Even when she had money, she would sometimes go without food simply because there was no one to fetch it from the market. With no man in the house, no son, who could bear the daily ordeal of cooking? For women, eating every day was not necessary. If she ate once, she could manage for two days without food. For the child, she would prepare fresh sweets or flatbreads when possible.

Under such conditions, how could her health not worsen? Worry, sorrow, and dire circumstances—all three plagued her simultaneously. And on top of everything, Nirmala had sworn not to take any medicine. After all, how could she afford it on those meager savings? When there was no certainty of food, how could she think of medication? Day by day, she withered away.

One day, Rukmini said, "Dear, how long will you keep wasting away like this? Life is the foundation of everything. Let me take you to the doctor."

With a tone of detachment, Nirmala replied, "If one has to live only to cry, then it's better to die."

Rukmini countered, "Calling for death won't make it come sooner."

Nirmala replied, "Death comes uninvited; why wouldn't it come when summoned? But it will take its time. The day I started this journey, count the years it has taken."

Rukmini consoled, "Don't lose heart, dear. You haven't even experienced the joys of this world yet."

Nirmala sighed, "If what I've seen so far is the joy of the world, I've had enough. Truly, sister, it's only my attachment to this child that keeps me bound here. Otherwise, I'd have left long ago. I shudder to think what fate holds for her."

The two women began to cry. Ever since Nirmala had been confined to her bed, Rukmini's heart had overflowed with compassion. There was no trace of bitterness left. Whatever she was doing, the moment she heard Nirmala's voice, she would rush to her side. She would sit by her for hours, narrating stories and scriptures. She would try to cook something Nirmala might enjoy. If she ever saw Nirmala smile, she felt elated. And as for the child, she treated her like a precious jewel, keeping her close at all times. The little girl had become the sole anchor of Rukmini's life.

After a pause, Rukmini said, "Why do you despair so much, dear? If God wills, you'll recover in a few days. Come with me today to the Doctor."

Nirmala replied, "Sister, no medicine or remedy will work for me now. Please don't worry about me. I entrust this child to your care. If she survives, please marry her into a good family. I could do nothing for her in my lifetime; I am guilty of only giving her birth. Whether you keep her unmarried or end her life, just don't tie her to an unworthy man. That's my only plea to you. I regret not serving you enough, and it grieves me deeply. No one found happiness through me. Whoever came into contact with me met ruin. If my husband ever returns home, tell him to forgive this wretched woman's sins."

Rukmini, crying, said, "Dear, you've committed no sin. I swear before God, I hold no ill will toward you. On the contrary, it's my deceit and duplicity toward you that will haunt me until my last breath."

Looking at her with tearful eyes, Nirmala said, "Sister, I shouldn't say this, but I can't keep it inside. My husband always doubted me, but I never disrespected him, not even in thought. What was meant to happen has already happened. Why would I do anything wrong and ruin my soul for the next life? Who knows what sins I committed in a previous life that I had to atone for in this one? If I had sown more thorns, where would I have ended up?"

Her breathing grew labored, and she lay back on the cot. She cast one final, profound glance at her daughter—an expression that conveyed the entire unspoken saga of her life. Words alone could not bear such weight.

For three days, tears streamed endlessly from Nirmala's eyes. She neither spoke nor looked at anyone, nor listened to anything. She simply wept. Who could fathom the depths of her anguish?

On the fourth day, at dusk, her sorrowful tale came to an end. Just as the birds returned to their nests, Nirmala's soul—wounded and weary from life's relentless trials—also took flight to its eternal abode.

The neighbors gathered. Her body was brought out. The question arose—who would perform the last rites? As people debated this, a frail old traveler arrived, carrying a small bundle. It was none other than Munshi Totaram.

www.ingramcontent.com/pod-product-compliance
Lightning Source LLC
La Vergne TN
LVHW010553160826
845677LV00013B/3109

* 9 7 8 8 1 9 6 2 2 6 4 9 7 *